Lotus Child

Jinna van Vliet

AuthorHouse™
1663 Liberty Drive, Suite 200
Bloomington, IN 47403
www.authorhouse.com
Phone: 1-800-839-8640

This book is a work of fiction. People, places, events, and situations are the product of the author's imagination. Any resemblance to actual persons, living or dead, or historical events, is purely coincidental.

© 2009 Jinna van Vliet. All rights reserved.

No part of this book may be reproduced, stored in a retrieval system, or transmitted by any means without the written permission of the author.

First published by AuthorHouse   5/7/2009

ISBN: 978-1-4389-6982-4 (sc)

Printed in the United States of America
Bloomington, Indiana

This book is printed on acid-free paper.

Dedication

First and foremost I dedicate this book to the Goddess Quan Yin whose gentle guidance has brought me to this stage in my life,

And I dedicate this story to the wounded child within all of us,

To the child who struggles to grow up,

To the child who only wants to be loved.

Acknowledgments

I would like to acknowledge the wonderful group who supported and encouraged me unfailingly as I walked along the painful pathways of memory lane.

First I would like to thank my husband Nico who washed the dishes and kept the house running while I hunkered before my computer for days and weeks.

With deep gratitude I thank the group of human angels who kept me going.

To Sonya my daughter who patiently sat with me and guided me through the confusing computer programs I was unfamiliar with.

To my friends Sylvia, Shelly, Caroline and Doreen who proof read my story page by page by page. And finally to Maureen, my editor friend. who never failed to come to my aid whenever I came knocking at her door.

I could not have done it without all of you.

I love you all dearly and thank you with all my heart.

Love Jinna

Table of Contents

Preface	xi

Part One   The Seed

Chapter One	1
Chapter Two	10
Chapter Three	18
Chapter Four	27
Chapter Five	36
Chapter Six	46
Chapter Seven	55
Chapter Eight	62
Chapter Nine	73

Part Two   The Seedling

Chapter One	81
Chapter Two	87
Chapter Three	96
Chapter Four	105
Chapter Five	115
Chapter Six	121
Chapter Seven	130
Chapter Eight	138

Part Three The Sapling Stalk

Chapter One	147
Chapter Two	160
Chapter Three	171
Chapter Four	178
Chapter Five	187
Chapter Six	194
Chapter Seven	200
Chapter Eight	208
Chapter Nine	221
Chapter Ten	229
Chapter Eleven	243
Chapter Twelve	251

Preface

I grew up with tales of magic and stories of heroes and heroines. Between my grandmother, my cousins and a number of my aunts I was constantly supplied with fantastic legends and fairytales of ancient China. As a child I was mesmerized and could not get enough of these entertaining stories. As I grew older I would often search through my cousin's trunk of old books and submerge myself for hours in a journey of fantasy.

LOTUS CHILD is the first book in the Lotus series and it is written as a fantasy interlude. I took the liberty of taking strands of my childhood years and strings of spiritual wisdom that I have accumulated and wove them all into a tale of a wounded child's journey into awareness of self.

LOTUS EMERGING is the second book and was published in 2006. This book was written as an autobiographical tale of emergence. It was an accounting of the spiritual journey we are all experiencing right now using my life as an example. It was a wonderful confirmation for me when a number of readers told me that they felt as if they were reading about their own life story.

The pending third book CRYSTAL LOTUS will be going into our ascension experiences a little deeper. It will contain the messages of the Goddess Quan Yin and her guidance to help us traverse the challenges of our Spiritual journey. Since the Harmonic Convergence we as humans have been on an incredible passage of spiritual discovery and awakening. Many channels have been sent to us to assist us at this time and Quan Yin is just one of the channels for the Divine Feminine. She brings us some of the tools we need to heal ourselves and to ease our transition in the physical, emotional and spiritual bodies as we head into the ascension process

We all have free choice and each choice is honored by the Divine Creator. There are many pathways to choose from and in the eyes of the Creator there are no wrong or right choices. It just IS A CHOICE.

I have chosen my path and present you with just one of the many choices available to everyone who wishes to boldly go where no human soul has gone before.

From my heart to yours.

Jinna

Part One

The Seed

*A memory awakened deep within the Lotus seed
There was a need to multiply, to grow
A sense of change, an awakening from cozy slumber
Cells shivering, dividing, multiplying, creating a new being
Tiny roots hesitantly sending tendrils out of its heart
Into a new environment full of challenges.
The seed remembered what it was before and knew its duty
It was time to emerge from the cocoon.
It was time to grow.*

Chapter One

In the small village of Sungai, the sun was just about to rise as it did every morning with the rooster's crow. Lowe the midwife groaned as she tried to cover her eyes to block out the bright beams of sunlight already streaming through the wooden window shutters.

"That's the price you pay when you live practically on top of the equator I guess," thought Lowe as she tried to ignore the explosion of sounds from at least a dozen roosters in the neighborhood. She was almost certain that the roosters must have agreed to compete as to who could beat the sunrise every morning!

About to raise herself to a seating position Lowe suddenly felt an unfamiliar jolt as if someone was prodding her with an electric wand. What in the ancestor's name was happening? A great sense of unease almost a painful sensation entered her belly. This was no ordinary sign, something was happening in the spirit world and being a medium, Lowe was very much attuned to the psychic energies around her.

Resigned that she was not getting out of bed yet, she fell back onto the firm mattress. She began to center herself with the balancing breath she was taught many years ago and allowed her mind to enter the stillness needed to enhance her intuitive sight. She was immediately flooded by waves of anticipation, of increased Light energy and the sense of great changes to come. A gateway into the ethers had been opened and something was changing in the energy fields around the village, perhaps the whole Universe itself! An uneasy sense of urgency enveloped her but before Lowe could find out more about it she was roughly brought back to awareness by an insistent knocking at her door. Lowe gave a deep exasperated sigh. Of all the luck someone had to come at this early hour.

"Aiiyah, I am coming, don't break my door down!" Lowe yelled out. Her irritation was evident in her use of the local vocal expression of annoyance or frustration depending on one's state of mind at the moment. As soon as Lowe tied her sarong more securely around herself she knew what the knock was all about. "She should know better", she berated herself; she had been expecting this call for the past few days. True enough before her stood one of the village maidens, jumping from one foot to the other in her excitement to deliver her message.

"Ibu, Ibu please come quickly. Apho's daughter is about to give birth. Come right now. Please hurry!"

The people in the community would always address her as 'Ibu' the word for esteemed Mother in the Malay language, showing the respect due to her station as the village mid-wife. After all she was instrumental in birthing every child under ten years old in this sleepy little tropical village. Lowe and her small circle of friends were members of a growing number of Descendents of Chinese traders who had sailed the trade winds from the Great Land Mass of China. Their Chinese dialect had permeated and usurped the local Malay dialect resulting in an interesting mix of vocabulary now used by the whole island.

Ibu thanked the girl and sent her back with the message that she would be there as soon as she could.

"There is still time anyway," Lowe mumbled to herself. "Lian loves attention and drama and she probably has the whole household in an uproar. And this is her fourth child for heaven's sake! Aiiyah, another grandchild for my poor friend Apho as if she didn't have enough mouths to feed." Lowe sighed deeply and began to prepare her birthing bundle of herbs. This activity made her forget the earlier incident that had awakened her.

It did not take Lowe long to walk down the dirt road towards Apho's home. There were only two paved roads that intersected creating a cross in the middle of the village. All other roads were actually dirt pathways. They were usually very dusty but a muddy nuisance during the rainy season! The village was surrounded by lush jungle growth. Roads and pathways were in constant need of clearing, otherwise the jungle would claim them back in an instant. Heavy foliage along the road was regularly in need of trimming even though most of the plants were displaying a variety of colorful tropical flowers like the hibiscus bush. Lowe always enjoyed the brilliant display of color but understood the necessity of pruning them down now and then. Besides, the village elders had been kind enough to tell her when the forest crews were about to do their work so that she could come and claim the cut branches. After all everyone in the village knew that a hibiscus plant had many medicinal properties when properly harvested and processed.

There was a lot of activity at the Liu household when the midwife arrived. Her friend Apho came hurriedly out of the birthing room to greet her.

"Thank the ancestors for coming right away Lowe. Lian does not have easy births as you well know but somehow this one seems to be more challenging for her. I don't know about you but I have been uneasy since her labor started last night. Are you sensing anything?"

"Now that you have brought it up, yes, I did feel something this morning."

Before Lowe could continue they were both interrupted by a loud moan coming from the room behind them. The two women entered the room and the midwife quickly approached the bed where Lian, Apho's youngest daughter was about to give birth. Lian was as unhappy as a wet cat; this was not a good time to have another baby. Her relationship with her husband was strained and a new baby would not help matters at all.

Quickly Lowe mixed some herbs together to ease the birthing process and not long after Lian had gratefully consumed the potion, she was able to move into the final birthing push.

"Thank you Lowe," Lian gasped, "I don't understand why the labor pains are more intense this time. I feel as if this child is fighting the birth! It must be a boy because all through my pregnancy this one had the strongest kicks!"

"Don't worry Lian," the midwife said soothingly, "You're doing just fine…it's all over now…here comes the baby!"

"Aiiyah she'll be screaming in disappointment this time!" The midwife whispered in dismay to her friend as she gently lifted the newborn from the exhausted mother.

"Yes, that's my daughter all right. I sometimes wish we had not spoiled her so after my husband died." The tired grandmother was suddenly interrupted by a frantic wail from the occupant of the bed.

"What are you two whispering about over there? Is it a boy? Tell me, tell me. It must be a boy. It has to be a boy! I prayed for a boy! I promised him a boy!!"

"As if the Goddess would hear your prayers girl!" Lowe mumbled under her breath. "You don't even believe in her and only pray to her if you want something. Spoiled girl!"

Apho was about to answer her daughter when she suddenly heard the midwife draw in a sharp breath and whisper, "Aiiyah this cannot be, after all these years! My eyes must be tired!"

"What is it Lowe, is something wrong with the child?" Apho's anxious voice sailed across the room

Lowe turned to face the startled grandmother. Cradling the softly crying newborn in her arms, she looked as if a bolt of lightning had just struck her head. Her eyes were wide, filled with shock, full of questions and apprehensive wonder. She did not answer immediately instead she pushed the flannel wrap open and gently exposed the baby's tiny chest. Bending her head closer to the child she peered at a tiny mark, which to the naked eye appeared to be a dot, a tiny birthmark.

Apho quickly took a step closer to find out what had startled Lowe so but was stopped in her tracks by the new mother's frustrated cry.

"What is wrong with you two? Mother, tell me is it a boy?"

"No, child," sighed her mother. "It is another girl."

"Another girl," shrieked Lian. "Another ugly girl! I don't want another girl! What am I supposed to tell him now?" Lian began to sob and moan, "Maybe she'll die just like cousin Mina's baby."

"Hush Lian, that is no way to talk about your new baby. I wish I had a baby girl. The Goddess gave me only two sons before my husband died. Can't you think how lucky you are for one moment and be grateful that God gave you three daughters!" Liamay, Lian's older sister who was assisting in the birth tried to console her sister even though she was exasperated with the new mother's complaints.

Apho looked helplessly towards the midwife and then to her hysterical daughter on the birthing bed. Liamay saw her mother's dilemma and came to the rescue. "It's all right mother. I'll look after Lian. You go ahead and find out if the baby's all right."

Apho turned her attention back to her friend who was still mesmerized by what she saw. "Lowe what are you staring at? You look as if you have seen a ghost. Is the child all right?"

"Have a look at this Apho. I am not sure what I am seeing. I sensed power when I guided the child out of the womb but did not realize what it was until I cleaned the baby."

"What is it?" Apho bent her head to peer at the tiny mark on the baby's chest. "It is just a dot, a birthmark, and a tiny one at that. Nothing to get upset about!"

"You don't understand. Go get the looking glass that makes things bigger, I know that you use one when you do your embroidery. Maybe your eyes will be able to see it then."

"Aiiyah! I still say that it's just a little round birth mark," grumbled Apho as she left the birthing room. She soon came back with her magnifying glass, a gift from one of her sons when he came back from the big city on the main island.

"Now let me see what you are talking about." Apho began to peer through the glass. "Am I seeing what I am seeing?" She gasped. Apho's pale shocked face looked up at her friend's similarly uneasy gaze. "Don't just stand there, tell me what you know!"

"The child needs feeding Apho. Let's just get the baby to the reluctant mother and then you and I need to have a very long talk."

"This is going to be a long day," Apho mumbled as she glanced at the new mother.

A few hours later, tranquility had finally descended over the Liu household and Liamay gently closed the door of the birthing room with a tired sigh. "They are both finally asleep," she announced as she walked into the living room.

It was a small room cozily furnished with four comfortably padded rattan chairs and a couple of small tables in between. There was a delicately carved china cabinet against one wall and another small table with flowering plants against the window. Lowe liked this room every time she came to visit. It had a warm welcoming atmosphere to it. She had seated herself comfortably with a cup of tea in her hand, and was smiling drowsily at Liamay. She had been awakened earlier than usual and had completely forgotten about breakfast.

"Mother will be right with you, she is just preparing the afterbirth."

"You are such a comfort to your mother Liamay. You carry a great amount of her burdens on your young shoulders. Why don't you start thinking of marriage again? You have been a widow for awhile now and you are still a very young woman. You deserve to find some happiness for yourself instead of catering to your sister's every whim. You have two young sons and yet you also look after your sister's children."

"They are no bother Auntie and I only look after the two older ones. They are about the same age as Sane, my youngest boy, so it is no trouble. Lian has her hands full already, especially now with the new baby, her fourth child. Luckily her third girl is such an angel. So quiet, she never gives her mother any trouble."

"That is the pretty one isn't she, Luan, isn't that right? I heard that she is your sister's favorite and Lian takes her everywhere she goes. A good thing really, that child will dedicate her whole life to Lian in payment of this special treatment she is getting now. They have a very unusual contract."

"You are a strange one Auntie, you scare me sometimes talking as if you can see the future. No, no, don't tell me anything about my life. I don't want to know! You know that I like you very much but I don't like the Dukun part of you. I get shivers every time I think of the things you can do! You get your rest and I'm going to get you something to eat." Waving her hands at Auntie, Liamay headed towards the kitchen.

Chapter Two

Apho walked into the room a moment later and overheard Liamay's departing words. "What was that all about?" she asked her friend curiously.

"It is just Liamay. You know how my psychic gifts scare her and she does not want to hear anything about the messages I get from the spirits. She is even reluctant to hear the voice of the Goddess."

"I don't know where she gets it from Lowe. You know that I believe strongly in the Goddess and the Spirits. I know that you are a powerful Dukun."

"Don't you try to get me irritated with that shamanic stuff. A Dukun is just a healer, you well know, a herbalist who helps the sick and not a dark witch who practices black magic!" Lowe raised her eyebrows and looked at her friend knowingly. "Liamay doesn't know that you are actually one of us does she?"

"No, and don't you tell her anything! I think that she must get this attitude of fear from my mother-in-law,"

Apho shook her head sadly and sighed again. It seemed as if the whole day was one big exasperated sigh. What a morning it had turned out to be!

"Aiiyah, you are probably right. Now sit down and join me in a cup of tea. While you and Liamay were busy cleaning up in there I took the liberty and brewed us a cup of my own special tea blend to help us face this new development."

With one more sigh Apho lowered her tired aching bones down into another comfortable rattan chair and gratefully accepted a cup from her friend. "Mmm, you put a dash of ginger and some lemongrass in this blend didn't you?"

"I should have known that you'd pick up on those two herbs, you just can't fool a knowledgeable herbalist."

"We can both finally relax and you had better start talking for your reaction to the baby has aroused my curiosity. I can hardly wait to hear all about it but first tell me that the child will be fine."

"She will be. Don't worry about that one. The mark of the Goddess is upon her. The Holy Goddess Quan Yin herself is overseeing the Light in this newest granddaughter of yours. How lucky can you get!! By the way you did save the afterbirth?"

"Yes, as soon as you told me the circumstances I knew that I had to save it. Am I right in assuming that we need to have a special ceremony when we bury the afterbirth?"

"You are right! You and I are to do a sacred ceremony at full moon for this one. Isn't it a noteworthy coincidence that the birth occurred exactly within the three days of the full moon? I tell you, the Goddess has something planned with this one. I wonder if the legend was true after all."

"What legend?" Apho exclaimed in surprise.

Before her friend could respond they were interrupted by the arrival of breakfast.

"Here you are, I brought a bowl for you too Mother". Liamay put two steaming bowls of rice porridge before the two elders. "I will have mine in the kitchen because I know that you two want to discuss this morning's events and I really don't want to know what it is all about!"

Both elders chuckled and settled themselves more comfortably in their chairs with their bowls of porridge and a cup of much needed tea as well. As they both began to eat, Auntie quietly began to gather her thoughts.

"I don't know much about it really. I heard my mother talking to my grandmother one day. You know that my grandmother just like your grandmother came from a remote mountainous region in central China. One reason that you also have the gift old friend, your mother was born there. You just choose to ignore it most of the time."

"Never mind about me. I am getting impatient. Tell your story! My granddaughter's life is at stake here."

"Tsk, tsk, how demanding you are today! Now then, when I was a young child I overheard my grandmother explaining something to my mother. At first it all sounded like a very interesting adventure story to me. My mother apparently heard a rumor about a child born in China, our homeland, with an unusual birthmark and wanted to know why the child was taken to the monks in the monastery right away.

My grandmother then proceeded to tell her this story. According to ancient legends, before the Goddess ascended back to the heavens, she promised to choose special children to be her emissaries to continue her work here on Earth. We would recognize these special children for they would carry the mark of the lotus on their heart. We all know that the Goddess is all about love, fertility and compassion and always encourages us to live our lives based on her teachings. As legends tell it, these children have special psychic gifts. They were to be born with special powers, which would surface once they were awakened into their awareness of the Goddess within them. We would recognize them by their intelligence, healing powers and the gift of spirit sight. Not many of these children have been sighted over the years and usually if there was one, the baby was immediately sent to be educated and trained by the monks. So far they have mostly been boy children. For some reason the Goddess must know that males carry more voice in this society of ours. The last one was found decades ago. Since then things have changed. and even the monks have forgotten most of the legends. I always thought that it was a very nice fairy tale. Leave it to my grandmother to continue the legends as told to her. My mother continued the tradition as bedtime stories. Well that was what I thought for a long time.

You know how I love the Goddess and have dedicated my life to her. I truly wished to believe in this legend. I wanted so much to be one of these special children that

I used to examine my chest in front of the mirror hoping to see a tiny lotus there! No luck there, never a mark not even a dot! I even used some dye and deliberately drew the symbol on my chest! Stop laughing! I know it was a silly thing to do!" Lowe joined in her friend's laughter as she recalled her own foolishness.

"Well, now you can imagine how I felt when I saw the dot on your granddaughter's chest. I somehow knew right away what it was because of the incredible energy it radiated. I had you bring the looking glass because I wanted to be sure and there it was, the tiniest most perfect of lotus blossoms. Did you see the tiny petals? It will grow a bit bigger of course as the child grows but it will always retain its perfect shape. I felt an amazing wave of love as the child was birthed. I should have known that it was an unusual occurrence if I had paid more attention and focused more on the joyful occurrence of a new birth instead of being irritated with your daughter's screams and curses. My other excuse was that I was also shocked at seeing the sign on a female child, which is unusual to begin with. I also noticed a faint pink glow of light out of the corner of my eyes and again did not pay attention until much later."

"A pink light? Where did it come from? I did not see anything!" Apho interrupted.

"Your emotions of worry and frustration were all over the place. No wonder you could not see it. It came from the Quan Yin statue that was in the corner altar in the birthing room. You know we always bring the Goddess in at every birthing; she is the Goddess of fertility after all. It sure filled me with awe seeing it glow; I have never seen this phenomenon in all the years that I have been a midwife. What a blessing the Goddess has bestowed upon this birth! I understand now what happened this morning," Lowe suddenly exclaimed. "I was trying to tell you when I came in."

"What's wrong? Did something happen to you this morning?"

"I was still half asleep this morning when it happened. I should have known that the spirits were trying to tell me something important. They were trying to give me all the clues and silly me, allowed the sound of the door knocking to distract my inner focus. I must be getting old! I used to be able to stay in a meditative state no matter what the outside distraction was!"

"You frighten me Lowe. I know you speak the truth but this message really scares me. What will happen to this child? What am I going to do with her? Aiiyah! What am I to tell Lian? What am I to do Lowe? Tell me, ask the Goddess, ask your guides, and ask all the spirits!" The old healer was quite agitated and fearful at this news.

"Calm down old friend, what does your heart tell you? You know that I look upon you as my sister for as I said before you have the same gifts as I do. You just chose to ignore them and have not taken the effort to allow them to grow. This is an opportunity for you to strengthen your connections to the Goddess. She knows your heart and sees the good deeds that you have done for this community. You have worked quietly in her name and let me tell you many will remember this in good time. I know how many owe you money and yet you have never tried to collect especially when you know how poor they are. She loves you very much and you know that!! So what do you want us to do? The decision is yours for you have been chosen to be the child's protector while she is in her most vulnerable early human stages."

"This is a hard decision to make. I don't know why but I feel very strongly that we have to keep this a secret. I cannot even tell Lian herself. What are you smirking at?"

"Not smirking dear sister, smiling, I am smiling! The Goddess is very happy with you and she has been standing with us all this time. She was whispering in your ear and she wants you to know how pleased she is that you are listening. She will walk with you more closely to help you with the child. You are the child's first mentor and guide. She will stay with you for her first five years of earth life."

"Aiiyah, no! Am I to lose her after five years? No, no, please Holy Goddess!" Apho pleaded.

"She is not going to die, silly! You know how this works. I feel for you and I know that it will hurt when the time comes but this child has a long road ahead of her. The time that she spends with you will sustain her and help her face the more difficult parts of her life. I will help you, together we will teach her and give her as many tools as we can to help her on her journey."

"What else, what else does the Goddess show you of her future Lowe?"

"It is enough for now Apho. She will show us more at a later time. She says that this is enough information for us right now. In our humanness we cannot always deal with the higher ways of the Goddess. Let us thank her for now and accept whatever information she is willing to share with us."

"Aiiyah, I will accept the Goddess' words. Please tell her how honored I am that she has chosen me. Between you and I though I am not sure that it is a good thing! Aiiyah, how is Kin, the father, going to react to all of this? I have warned Lian over and over not to marry him! He is a spoiled brat, a no-good father. He does not even pay any attention to his only son! And he wants more sons! Do you know that he has barely paid me enough for food for the children while they are living with me?"

"It's all right. Don't get yourself all worked up again! Control your emotions and remember the teachings of the Goddess. She is all about love and compassion to all beings and yes even to that son-in-law of yours! He is a soul of light in human form just like all of us. And don't forget that this child is blessed by the Goddess herself.

Let's discuss what we need to do next. Tomorrow the moon will show her full face. Come to my house then for the ceremony with the afterbirth. I will prepare everything else. Amazing isn't it how the timing is just perfect. Born within the three day period of a full moon, in the ninth month, the month dedicated to all the Goddesses and also in a nine year number! I am just a bit puzzled as to the day though, it should have been a day later. I'll have to ask my spirit guides a number of questions next time. The Goddess knows what she is doing so stop worrying!"

Chapter Three

Two days later as the sun hovered low on the horizon it cast a golden orange-red glow over a small figure walking down the pathway towards the midwife's humble home. The evening star was already shimmering behind the spectacular colorful display of the setting sun. The star's presence is the signal to all the night creatures to prepare their vocal instruments to welcome the queen of night. The sounds of the crickets tuning their instruments were everywhere.

"Lowe are you there, are you home?"

"Of course, where else would I be? You ask the same question every time you come to visit. I was expecting you after all." Chuckling and shaking her head at her friend Lowe motioned her in. "Did you bring it?"

"Talking about repetitions, there you go again, of course I did. Didn't you trust me not to forget? I am not that old yet you know! I may be older than you but not senile yet!"

Lowe chuckled again as she turned towards the tea table. The midwife's humble home was a small cottage with a couple of bedrooms and a small adequate kitchen. A cozy living area next to the kitchen was where the ever present tea table was kept and where the two friends were now sitting.

"How are mother and child? Oh, oh, here it comes don't start the tears yet old friend. We need a positive, loving energy to do this work tonight. Aiiyah, let's get it over with. I knew something was not quite right with the energies surrounding the child last night. What happened?"

I am so angry at both of them!" And I blame myself for not being there in time to protect the child." Apho was seething with anger and indignation.

"Whatever it is, it is not your fault Old One. Was the child hurt? Mind you the Goddess told me that she was all right. Out with it what on earth happened?"

"You know that every time she has a baby, he leaves and does not come home until everything is over. Well this time he took his time and did not come home until last night. I did not know this until afterwards but apparently one of our well-meaning neighbors came to visit earlier in the day, to see the baby. She told Lian that her husband saw Kin in the city at a party well attended by prostitutes. You and I know that Pankal is filled with these houses of ill repute. You have noticed often enough how jealous Lian can be. That gossip threw her into a temper tantrum. Liamay and I tried to calm her down and we thought that we were successful. Ahhhh, why didn't I see it coming?" Apho lamented as she bowed her head sorrowfully. "We heard him come home after supper and then the screaming started. Liamay and I rushed to their room to get the baby but by that time it was too late. Lian in a fit of rage, threw the baby at his feet!"

"Aiiyah, she didn't! Is the baby hurt?" Lowe gasped.

"I don't think so, thank the ancestors! The Goddess must have whispered something in my ear again because I insisted that Lian wrap the baby in an extra blanket to keep her warm that morning. I made sure that she was really bundled up tightly. I think that this cushioned the baby's fall. She has good lungs though. You should have heard her scream when she hit the floor!"

Apho smiled proudly for a moment at the memory of a little red face, tiny dark brown eyes full of outrage and the rose-bud mouth wide open in full protest at this outrageous treatment. How can Lian call her own baby ugly? Hah, in my opinion she is the most beautiful baby girl ever born. Well of course that is a biased opinion of a doting grandmother."

Lowe sighed with relieve. "Thank the Goddess! She sure chose a couple of very strong influences as parents for the little one," she continued. "It almost feels as if this is the beginning of an acceleration of the flow of spiritual growth for this child. Aiiyah, in a way I feel sorry for the girl. It is not going to be easy!"

Lowe turned towards the window as she noted the brightening beams of moonlight flooding the room and got up to get ready. "Let's get started as the moon is almost at its highest journey in the sky."

Both elders began to loosen their hair from its constricted bun. In their generation all married women had to wear long hair that had to be twisted in a bun at the back of the head called a kunde. Next they donned their ceremonial loose shifts. Both their shifts were made out of cotton fiber. They were identical but Apho had skillfully decorated each with different embroidered patterns at the neckline and the hem. Lowe's was a red shift decorated with a white and gold pattern symbolizing her status as a healer and as a handmaiden of the Goddess. Apho had chosen to embroider her favorite rose pattern intertwined with a soft green garland of herbs on her green shift.

As soon as they were gowned Lowe quickly gathered her medicine bundle that she had prepared earlier and the two elders quietly went into the garden. The garden was completely fenced in and could only be entered through a gate at the back of the house.

Lowe headed towards the corner where she had erected a small stone altar. It was positioned in such a way that during a full moon a moonbeam would shine directly into its center. This was Lowe's sacred place where she could do her sacred ceremonies. The village people were very nervous about witch doctors and would shun her if they knew what she was capable of doing. They knew her as the village healer, the midwife, and Apho's friend. Apho, was also known, loved and respected just as much, and also addressed as Ibu as she walked the village as a healer, the other wise woman herbalist.

The moon was so bright that the trees and bushes were casting eerie shadows all around them. As the women approached the altar, both noticed how quiet the night seemed. The evening sounds of crickets and other animals on any given tropical full moon night were very loud. However after the initial sounds earlier they were suddenly strangely absent. There was an odd sense of anticipation as if the whole world was holding its breath. As they approached the altar, Lowe began to chant softly, inviting the energy of the Goddess to draw nearer. They were waiting for the precise moment for a moonbeam to reach the center of the altar where five white quartz crystal stones were arranged in a star pattern. As the moon continued to rise towards its highest point, Apho placed a small dish of seawater, a white water lily to represent the lotus and the small bundle that contained the afterbirth in the center of the star pattern.

A soft warm wind began to whisper around them and the shadowy trees began to sway to the gentle cadence of the chant. The moon blessed the scene with her pearly gaze.

Continuing their chant in a soft sing-song voice both women were now in a deep meditative state, reaching the balance needed to open the gateway of communication with the Goddess. Soon the moment was upon them and an iridescent white beam reached the altar, activating the stones, engulfing all the objects in the center and at the same time encapsulating both women in its brilliant light. Anyone present at that moment would have noticed three columns of light manifesting behind the altar before the two human figures as the five stones ignited and began to glow. Five golden white lines erupted from the crystals, connecting, forming a pentagon, the five pointed star of the Goddess. Time stood still, a still point as if the Universe held its breath for an infinite moment. Then a faint sound of chimes, the sweet scent of tropical blossoms and the moon resumed her journey of light across the heavens.

"Holy Goddess," Lowe whispered in awe as she turned to look at her partner.

Wide eyes on a pale face gazed back at her and Lowe had to nudge her friend gently to remind her to complete the ceremony. With trembling fingers Apho took the small bundle from the altar and lovingly laid it in the minute grave that Lowe had prepared earlier in the day. Both began to chant the thanksgiving song while carefully putting the lily on top of the bundle. Then they gently sealed the grave by scooping the dirt with their hands and patting it reverently into a tiny mound. Continuing the chant they washed their hands in the sea water and then sprinkled the water over the mound. Bowing respectfully towards the altar, both backed away three paces before turning around and leaving the moon bathed garden. Both were speechless with awe and wonder.

On cue suddenly the familiar night songs of the crickets erupted all around them as if a joyful orchestra decided to pay tribute to the occasion.

Back at the house, both collapsed in their chairs, each trying to absorb the enormity of the experience for a long moment. After awhile Lowe got up to put the kettle on for tea. Turning to her friend she said, "I hope you saw and heard everything that happened tonight or I will begin to think that I am crazy! I have never had anything happen like this with any of the afterbirth ceremonies I have performed!"

"What on the ancestor's breath happened back there Lowe? I felt as if I was granted a glimpse of heaven! The music, the feeling of bliss and I could even smell the flowers. I don't know what kind, I just know that I wished I could have my hands on a drop of that essence. What did you get out of it? Who were those spirits of Light? I recognized the Goddess, well I think I did! Who are the other two? I sensed so much power there." Still in the aftermath of shock, Apho shuddered at the memory of it.

"That is exactly what I felt too. Aiiyah, we have been blessed, what an unexpected honor for both of us. You are right for the pink one was our beloved Goddess Quan Yin, radiating a powerful pink love chi. As to the other two, I am not sure if I heard it correctly since the voice was so loving and gentle but this is what I sensed. Quan Yin kept addressing the white one as mother and the ice-blue one as sister. Did you see the brilliant white lightning bolts that radiated out of the mother? Well it looked like lightning bolts to me! Now the pearly blue one I recognized, it was the Holy Moon Goddess herself! Did you see her floating down one of the moonbeams? She is so beautiful, in her full-moon regalia as she glided down toward us on a shimmering moonbeam. I always wish that I could one day buy a cloth with that iridescent silvery blue color! I can't wait to connect with my spirit guides as I am very curious to know why they came!"

"I remember trying to shade my eyes because the mother was so bright, she almost looked like a silver spider woman don't you think? And the presence of the Moon Goddess as well, Aiiyah what an honor."

"Now that you mention it, you are right Old One, the mother being looked like a big bright spider with a woman's body. I am getting very inquisitive! The Goddess called her mother so she must be the mother of all the Goddesses! We should address her as mother as well when we see her again."

"I am not sure I want to see her again Lowe! She is a very powerful being and I feel very unworthy to be in her presence. The Goddesses must have something big in store for my grandchild for three of them to show up like that. What are they grooming her for? It really frightens me when I think of all this!"

"Well stop thinking about it. The first note has been entered in the first page of her book of life tonight and it will be part of the life challenges she has to overcome. When Lian threw her down before the father it created a big stamp in the book. A stamp of rejection, of being unaccepted, unloved by the parents, the very human guardians she has chosen. Aiiyah, what a list this one is going to have to overcome!"

"What else did you hear? I was so stunned and even being in a meditative state it was still overpowering. I don't think I'll ever forget this night."

"There was just a great sense of joy and honor. They have been waiting for this child for a long time. Now we'll just have to take it one day at a time and try to keep the child safe. The most important thing is to show her how much we love her. Knowing that she is loved is vital for this child, especially now that the first difficult entry has been written in her book."

"Not an easy job, not an easy one at all," Apho groaned.

Chapter Four

Six months have gone by since the eventful birth. The Liu family weathered the ups and downs of the family circle and matters were relatively calm until the next disruption which would shatter the peace again. It seemed that a truce did not last very long for their family.

"Oh stop crying Ayin! What's wrong with you?!" cried Lian in exasperation and impatience.

"Stop shaking that child Lian!" Apho intervened as she hurried through the doorway and reached out for the sobbing child, taking her out of her irate mother's arms.

"She's only six months old you are expecting too much of her."

"Luan never gave me any trouble when she was a baby. She never cried like this one. I knew that this one was trouble the moment I looked into her eyes. There is something strange about this one. I swear that sometimes she does not look at you like a baby! I don't know what it is but she makes me feel uncomfortable every time she looks at me. Are you hiding something from me Mother? Is there something about this child that makes her look at me that way? That reminds me, what were you and Auntie Lowe hiding from me? You never told me what happened in the birthing room that morning."

Apho sucked in a startled breath and quickly assessed the situation. She had better come up with something very fast. Aiiyah, of course, she did have something to tell Lian about the child, she sighed with relieve. "Have you noticed her neck Lian?"

"What's wrong with it?"

"Did you have a good look at it? Aiiyah, I thought so, you have barely paid attention to this daughter, and you rarely bathe her."

"I can't help it," Lian grumbled. "She is a difficult baby and cries all the time no matter what I do!"

"Look here," Apho gently lifted Ayin's chin causing the child to giggle and squirm in her arms. It was interesting how Ayin seemed to settle down immediately when she was out of her mother's arms.

"What happened, what are those red lines on her neck?"

"Lowe says that the umbilical cord was wrapped pretty tight around her neck, which is why Ayin did not cry right away if you recall."

"Is it dangerous? Is it affecting her brain, her growth or something else? What will happen to her? That's all I need, a child with brain damage!"

"No it is not dangerous but Lowe says that she might develop thyroid problems in her later life."

"Oh well that is a long way from now. She is already a strange looking child any way. Just look how white her skin is, there is barely any color to it! If she did not have those Chinese eyes and the straight black hair, people would think that she was fathered by a white man. The other children all have such nice light brown skin but this one had to be different! Aunty Thina even called her 'Whitey' the other day. What did I do to deserve such an odd child?"

"There is nothing wrong with her skin. It is such a soft white skin, almost translucent. I think it is pretty myself, unusual, yes but pretty."

"Anything about that child you think beautiful Mother. I don't understand why you just dote on this odd one. By the way Mother," Lian looked beseechingly at her mother. "She is weaned. I have not given her the breast for a few days now and she seems to take to the bottle easily enough. Can you look after her for awhile?"

"As you wish she'll sleep with me from now on", and with that Apho turned and carried the now drowsing baby into her room. A small smile of satisfaction lingered around Apho's lips. "Good, now the child will be truly safe!" she whispered to herself.

Lian heaved a sigh of relief. The child had caused a wedge between herself and her husband and it did not sit well with her. Now she could manipulate and plan in her subtle ways to woo him back into her bed. It had been too long and knowing him that was an excuse to start looking for other flowers of the night. After all, the fact that she was the acclaimed beauty of the village was the reason he fell in love with her and she still had her figure despite birthing four children. People still considered her a beauty and she was certain that she could still get his attention with her pretty face.

The move did not affect Ayin at all and both grandmother and child had an excellent night. For the next few weeks, the Liu household was running at a more tranquil pace in spite of the four children and a crawling baby.

Another sunny day arrived and Apho quickly completed her chores that morning. She looked forward to these rare, precious moments when she could detach herself for a little while from all the troubles and worries of her family. "Liamay I am on my way now, keep an eye on Ayin please. She is very inquisitive and is crawling all over the place."

"Don't worry, Mother. You really spoil that girl too much! It is as if she is the only granddaughter you have, really! With you picking her up constantly it's a wonder if the child will ever learn to walk! Now get going, you deserve a rest from this place, go have your regular cup of tea with Auntie Lowe".

"If you only knew," mumbled Apho as she closed the gate behind her.

It was such a beautiful sunny day again. "How could anyone not be filled with gratitude to the Earth Mother," the old woman thought as she breathed in the scents of nature around her. Walking along the path, her eyes darted here and there paying attention to the greenery around her. Once in a while she would stop and stoop to gather some herbs growing among the stones. It was always a good idea to pick more herbs even though she had a good stock already. One never knew when there would be another fever outbreak like last year. The tiny bushes gave the best results when picked fresh after a gentle rain, like the one last night that cleansed the dust from every bush and blade of grass. It made the lush green vegetation appear so vibrant, sparkling with the life essence of nature itself. The old woman chuckled to herself as she found another patch of the fever herbs right at Lowe's gate. She could hardly wait to tell her friend, the midwife, what was right on her doorstep! "Look what you missed Old Witch," she teased her friend as she walked into the cottage.

"Aiiyah, wait until I find things around your house!" Both laughed at that probability.

"How is our girl?" was Lowe's first question as soon as the two elders were comfortably settled in their chairs with a cup of fragrant tea.

"Mmm…dandelion root and a dash of liquorish bark to sweeten the bitterness?"

"Not many can fool your taste buds, can they?" Her friend chuckled, confirming Apho's guess.

"Ayin is much better now," The old healer answered Lowe's inquiry. "She really blossomed as soon as I took her away from her parents' bedroom. Lian barely notices her absence and rarely bothers to ask about her youngest daughter. I noticed pinch marks on her little arms the other day and it really upset me, I could almost feel the hurt myself. Every time I confront Lian we end up in a shouting match. Sometimes I wish they would move and live in their own home but leave Ayin with me. How can my own daughter treat her own offspring this way? Where have I gone wrong Lowe?"

"You have not done anything wrong, Sister. Stop feeling guilty, it does you no good. It will only make you sick. And then who is going to look after Ayin? You know that they have no money to move. You are the one who has been supporting the whole family since the babies began arriving. This is just another entry in the child's book of learning. The problem with abuse is that it lingers for years, festering and causing deep wounds in one's emotional body. I just pray that Ayin will get a lot of help with this lesson. I know and understand that the Goddess will help her but ultimately she is the one who has to make the choice to heal it or not in this lifetime."

"You said that she carries a part of the Goddess. Does that not immediately give her the power to heal anything thrown at her in this life? She won't remember, will she? After all she is only a baby right now," Apho anxiously appealed to her friend.

"No she won't remember these incidences. The energy of them will still be there in her emotional body and when the abuse continues the wound builds up like a pile of dirt. As to your other question, that's the strange twist that happens when a soul incarnates into a human body. The human body is like an empty house. Then a soul comes in as the housekeeper. We are the housekeepers. Special spirits who are part of the soul family will choose to come in and live in different rooms of the house as part of a contract with the housekeeper.

Now once in a while, a higher spirit like one of the Goddesses will come in. This is what is happening with your granddaughter. You see the housekeeper is the one who has to do all the cleaning and looking after the house. The cleaner the rooms the stronger, bigger parts of the spirits can come in. They cannot live in dirty rooms and by dirt I mean all the heavy negative emotions that we humans are subjected to in this earthly life. The Goddesses are spirits of very high vibrating light beings and require big clean rooms. It is a lot of work and it takes a lot of energy to get these rooms clean."

"I don't understand God and His Goddesses really I wish they would not make things so complicated."

"By the way did you pick up on the clue that the Goddess has given this child?" Lowe asked as she changed the subject.

"What clue?" Diverted from her painful thoughts, Apho turned a puzzled look at her friend as she took a sip from her cup. "By the way this is a really good cup. If I didn't know you better I would think that you had stolen one of my herbal recipes," Apho teased her friend again.

"Me steal your recipes, you wish! Back to the clue, you did not see it?"

Apho shook her head and continued to look puzzled.

"Tell me who named the child?"

"You know that the father did. Kin always insists that he name all his children. He wants people to know that they are the fruit of his loins, his! Aiiyah! He does not even spend time with any of them but treats them like property." Apho shook her head in disgust. "Now, what's wrong with my granddaughter's name?"

"You are not saying it right. Now say it slowly the way it sounds in our native tongue."

"Aaah – Yin. Aiiyah," gasped Apho as the significance dawned on her. "The Goddess sure knows how to hide her name, doesn't she?"

Suddenly Apho bursts into peals and peals of laughter. This time it was Lowe's turn to look puzzled.

"What, what? What did I miss?"

"Kin, the father, he has no idea that he has just satisfied the Goddess' plans, doesn't he! And he does not even believe in the Goddess! He proudly told everyone that he had done the research and picked out special names for his daughters. He found them in an ancient Chinese text and they are names of flowers and jewels in the ancient tongue. That's what he claims anyway!"

At that Lowe joined her friend in relieved laughter. "What a joke that was on this man!"

Lowe suddenly fell silent, her eyes glazed over and her arms dropped like limp noodles onto her lap. Startled, Apho immediately leaned forward, closing the gap between them. She had learned to recognize the sudden change in the midwife when the Goddess decided to communicate directly through her. Her friend was a powerful medium and Apho did not want to miss anything this time, intuitively realizing that it would have something to do with Ayin's name. Lowe's breathing slowed down significantly.

Then without warning a soft voice floated out of her slightly open mouth as the Goddess took over her human vocal cords.

"Many more parts will be added to the child's name. As she awakens many earth years from now, she will recognize and accept the other parts of her name. Each part will open the doors to awareness of who she truly is. As she begins to accept her destiny she will be our gift to all women who choose to answer our call of awakening. We are very pleased with the work that both of you have done. Know that we will walk with you and assist you in this earthly journey. Our love will continue to shine upon both of you."

Lowe sighed deeply, straightened her back and blinked her eyes open. "Aiiyah, I hope you remembered that entire transmission. She does not always allow me to remember the messages when she channels through me like this. What did she say, what did she say?"

Tears began to flow from Apho,s eyes as she repeated the message.

"I don't understand the whole message and I am afraid Lowe, I am truly afraid for this child. What kind of game are the Goddesses playing here? I just don't understand any of this."

"Ours is not to question why dear sister. We are merely human mortals and women like you and I have chosen to give our life to do the work of the Goddess. Remember what I told you earlier, we're just the housekeepers. Trust and have faith Old One and that is all we can do in this short life of ours."

Chapter Five

Two more months had passed and the Liu family continued to experience the turbulent relationship issues with each other. Living together as an extended family provided each member with many challenges, particularly for the two adults who seemed to be the only ones able to keep the family on an even keel. At least, the mother and elder daughter team of Apho and Liamay had been successful in keeping the children fed and happily unaware of the frequent emotional confrontations that the adults had to face.

Another dawn and Grandmother Apho could feel the strands of tension among the family members already. She knew in her old bones that it was going to be one of those challenging days. Would there be any day where her sighs could be for happiness and contentment at all? Why is life sometimes so painful? Something did not seem right and she wondered where her younger daughter was. "Liamay, where is Lian? I haven't seen her all day. As a matter of fact I have not seen Luan either."

"I tried to talk her out of it Mother, but she is so stubbornly jealous and has a one-track mind when it comes to that husband of hers."

"What did she do now?!" asked an exasperated Alpho.

"She took Luan with her and hitched a ride to the city. She found out again that Kin has gone to one of his rich friends' private parties. Everyone knows that Kin and his so-called friends have these big parties in Pankal and of course it always involves a number of those beautiful women!" Liamay rolled her eyes in exaggerated disgust. . .

"I don't know how to talk to your sister any more! Sometimes I feel as if I have lost my youngest daughter. It seems like it was just yesterday that she came home from the white man's college on the main island. How proud we were of her certificate! Remember the plans we had then? How she was going to start her dressmaking business and how we were all going to help by generating clients for her. You and your brothers put up the initial cost for the enterprise and it was very successful. She even had the Mayor's wife ordering clothes from her! Aiiyah! Look at her now! She has not touched her sewing machine since her wedding day!"

"She got her head turned when he started paying attention to her, the first time they met at Uncle Bonay's party, remember? Unfortunately, you and I were not there mother. Besides I am not sure that we could have prevented Lian from falling in love with him. Which young girl wouldn't be attracted to the oldest son of the Bune family, a family considered to be one of the richest households in the village? They own the only gas station in town besides shares in the tin mines on top of all their other businesses in town."

"Spoiled rotten that's what he is!" Apho grunted disgustedly.

"Lian was the prettiest unmarried girl in town those days and he was considered the most desirable matrimonial catch as you recall."

"Well I never liked him, even then! Especially when I saw him roar around the village with his motorcycle, not caring when he showered everyone on the road with all that dust. He was such a show-off because he knew that he was the only young man who owned a motorbike! Furthermore he behaved as if he was the only one in town who was smart, just because his father had the money to send him to Singa. I heard that he learned the other white man's language there - the one called English. Pah! It makes me sick just talking about it!" Apho was working herself up into a frustrated disgruntled state.

"It is all water under the bridge, Mother. It is no use crying over it. They are all living here now and you are feeding the whole family. Why don't you demand that he pay more to help with the household expenses?"

"You know that his family disowned him when he left his father's house and came to live here. Besides, he did help us when the war was on. He did get us flour and sugar when it was short in supply everywhere. No one could even buy any remember?"

"Tch! That was sheer luck that the Japanese Captain liked him and gave him extra supplies for the seniors' home!"

Mother and daughter looked at each other and they both started to giggle at the same time, while remembering the incident that perpetrated the much-needed windfall. Both began to reminisce at the same time, recalling the sequence of events.

"I don't understand what the war was all about, but I have never seen him so frightened in my life. I even hoped that it might make a man out of him," Apho remarked.

"The Japanese occupation was very frightening Mother. It was downright horrible! The rumors about rapes and pillaging by the soldiers were all over the village and we were both terrified. They were also looking for all the young men ever since they took over the running of the island. Nobody knew what they were going to do with the men, but everyone knew what happened to the Dutch Mayor and his family. I hoped that they did not suffer too much for too long. What was done to them was hideous and very cruel."

"Yes, I agree with you there. My heart wept for them when I saw how they were chained and marched out of the village. I heard later that many of them who were taken as prisoners of war had died, but that the survivors had to march through the jungle for days. This must have been a very big war in the outside world, if the enemy would even bother taking over such a small village like ours! I had never met a Japanese person until that time. Mind you, they were all soldiers and no matter what country they belong to, they are all trained killers, as far as I am concerned."

"You are right, Mother. They called this the Second World War and it involved many countries in the world. I had been listening to Uncle Bonay's radio when the news came through that this awful war was finally over. The American people had to take a horrendous step to end it. I am glad they did, because those Japanese soldiers were nasty to us too. I don't care if they were killer soldiers or not, but I am still very angry at what one of their Captains did to second cousin, Moi!."

"Hush Liamay, your uncle had no choice. His life and your aunt's life were at stake. He had to agree to give Moi to the captain."

"But she was only a child Mother, not even fourteen yet! I heard that he raped her repeatedly! Look at her now, only fifteen and already a mother with a baby! I don't think that I can ever forgive these Japanese soldiers for what they did!"

"I know that it is hard to forgive something like that, child, but the Goddesses have told us repeatedly that we must always forgive, even though we do not understand the whys about it."

"I don't care anymore what the Goddesses said; they don't have to endure these atrocious things here on Earth. I heard that this Second World War had hurt many other people very badly too, especially the people they call the Jews. The German army had done worse things to these people, so I guess I should be thankful that most of us in the village did not suffer too much at the enemy's hands. I still think that the Goddesses are asking too much of us when it comes to forgiving though."

Apho ignored her daughter's last rebellious statement and continued the conversation, "Second World War, huh and we didn't even know that there had been a first one. What a strange world we live in! Best not to talk about it any more. As they say, bad things will get worse if you keep talking about it! Getting back to Kin, what happened out there in the jungle? You and Lian and the children went with him when he decided to go into hiding."

"Nothing much really. Of course, he expected to be served in the same manner by all of us women! Someone betrayed him and he was shaking in his boots when the Japanese soldiers found him and escorted him back to their captain. Lian, of course was into the drama and collapsed in a fearful lump, moaning and wailing that he would be killed!"

"Sometimes I wish he was!" Liamay thought bitterly.

"I am glad that you went with her then. How I wished that I was a mosquito on the wall when I heard that he was brought before that Captain."

"Really Mother!" Staring at each other, they both burst out in giggles again.

"To be so fearful and then to find out that all the Captain wanted to do was to thank him! Funny how the Captain found out that Kin was the one who had been delivering extra rations to the seniors' home."

"Aiiyah! Of course, he was the only one whose truck was still running, because his father owned the gas station! He did not tell the Japanese of course, that it was you mother, who insisted that we help the elderly. And it was you who got Lian to persuade him to do it!"

"Well, it turned out to be beneficial for everyone in the end, because the Captain gave Kin extra rations for the seniors' home and we were able to get some extras too!"

"Lian had a great time playing the great and generous lady, didn't she? I watched her handing out small bags of sugar and flour to everyone who came to the door! You and I were the ones doing all the work Mother and she was playing the grand heroine!" Liamay could not hide her anger this time.

"Ah, Liamay, let it be. Let your sister have her fun. You and I would not enjoy all that bowing and thanking. Most of the time it was not a sincere act of gratitude anyway, look what is happening now. Those people who received the gifts have already forgotten who helped them to survive the times of food shortages in a war that we don't understand. No one in the village knows what it was all about and why the Japanese came to take over our little Island home. I am just glad that this strange war is over and I hope that we'll never have another one."

It was one of those hot, humid tropical afternoons and Liamay happened to turn towards the window hoping for a cool breeze when she noticed a familiar figure approaching the house. "Well, I'll be a tiger's cub!" she exclaimed in surprise. "Mother, look who is coming down the lane way."

Apho looked up from her needlework and abruptly got to her feet, spilling her spools of thread on the floor in her haste.

"It's Lowe! What in the Ancestor's name is going on? Something must have disturbed her, for she has always refused to come for a social visit ever since your sister and her husband moved in here." Apho opened the door right away and waved her friend in with a welcoming smile.

"Come in, come in Honored Dukun. What brings you to the neighborhood? How did you know that I had just finished baking your favorite coconut cookies?"

"Stop that! Honored Dukun, indeed!" The midwife glared at the two giggling women. "Now coconut cookies that's the way to welcome a tired and hungry guest after a walk in this hot steamy weather. How did you know I needed something to cheer me up this afternoon?"

"You're not the only one who needs a pick-me-upper my friend. Liamay and I just had a depressing chat about the war."

Without further ado, both elders settled themselves on the back porch in the welcome shade of the old mango tree. Liamay quickly brought them their tea and a plate of her mother's famous coconut cookies, still warm from the oven and then she left the two old friends alone.

Despite the sense of uneasy disturbances around Lowe, Apho insisted that she have at least three cookies and a few sips of herbal tea before speaking of whatever troubled her. Something must have happened in the village, or with one of Lowe's many grandchildren, Apho thought and was therefore unexpectedly surprised when her friend's opening question was, "How is Lian feeling these days?"

"Now why did you ask that? For that matter, why did you come here out of the blue, when I know that you do not like the energy of my son-in-law? Aiiyah! Did you get another message from the Goddess?"

"I had to come to find out, when I felt a disturbance in the grid surrounding your grandchild. Something has happened that will have a major impact on Ayin's future life."

"Out with it Old Friend - don't leave me in suspense. I get this uncomfortable jiggly feeling in my stomach every time you talk about the grid. I don't pretend to know anything about it and I don't want to know, but it does worry me."

"You might as well know that Lian is pregnant again."

"What! So soon after all the trouble she went through! Another child? Ayin is barely eight months old! Aiiyah! Don't tell me that the Goddesses are sending us another special one!"

"No Old One, not to worry, this one is not like Ayin. Actually, I am filled with sorrow when I think of this girl." Lowe shook her head sadly.

"Aiiyah! No, no, no! Not another girl! He wants another son, remember and I think that would be the reason for her to get pregnant again. They cannot afford more children! When are they going to stop? Now what is going to be wrong with this one? The way you rushed out here, tells me that there is more to this!".

"This one, the Goddess calls the buffer, the peacemaker, and the one who will call upon herself to take on the overflow of the troubles that will be directed towards Ayin. This one will be the forgotten one and also the one who sacrifices herself continually to keep peace in the family. This is a beautiful soul who has volunteered to take on this job and will gain many halos when she gets back to the Angelic World."

"Earth Mother help us! What kind of a life will this child have?"

It was not an easy message for the Old Healer to hear. She loved all her grandchildren although she did have her favorites. It pains the loving grandmother to think that any of her grandchildren would suffer in life.

"A most traumatic and difficult one my friend," Lowe shook her head somberly as her friend stared at her in horror. "That is why she will be rewarded in a big way when she returns home in the heavens. She will receive some help from many sources but this one can be very stubborn and her ego self will often refuse the helping hand."

Chapter Six

One year later, another life had joined the Liu household and the two old friends were in Lowe's house once more.

"What's happening with the new baby Old One? And how is our Little One doing?" The midwife inquired as the two friends settled in their chairs for their regular tea ritual.

Apho heaved a big sigh. This was but one in a long chain of sighs again! "For the life of the Goddess, I cannot remember any longer the times where I did not have to sigh in frustration or sadness. Since Suni's birth, Lian has practically forgotten Ayin, except for the times when the child has irritated her. I still cannot stop her from physically punishing the child. Lian has never spanked any of her children, but is somehow determined to remedy the situation with Ayin. Yet that little girl comes back again and again, and acknowledges her mother with loving gestures. Aiiyah! How can I protect that child?

She is so active and creative. She continually asks questions and wants to know everything, as well as why things are done the way they are." Apho chuckled as she recalled some of her favorite granddaughter's antics. "She is two years old, but already shows how smart she is." The proud grandmother smiled as she pulled out a piece of paper from her waist-pouch to show her friend. "Look at what she can do. I know it looks like a bunch of scribbles to you, but she told me what she was trying to draw. It was wet and miserable that day, with the monsoon rains pelting the roof and drenching the garden with torrents of water. All the children were bored and fidgety. Liamay had enough on her hands trying to keep the older children entertained, so I gave Ayin a piece of paper and some pencils to keep her occupied. Amazing how that child can focus at such a young age, once she is interested in something. She brought the paper to me saying that she made something for me and I asked her what she had drawn. Imagine her answer, "It's the rain Pho-Pho," she said, "See, it's making puddles and there are pretty colors in the puddles". As I told you before, she was very quick in learning how to talk and has called me Pho-Pho, our dialect for 'grandmother' very early. I have never heard her use baby talk the way the other children do at that age."

Lowe admired the piece of artwork with a chuckle. "You are right. It is quite the accomplishment for a child that age. However, I know that you have more news. I can feel it in my bones!"

"Oh! You and your bones, don't give me that excuse! You can see more through your little finger than any Dukun I know!"

Both ladies giggled and chuckled at that.

"Well as I told you last year, my number two son has finally gotten Kin a proper job with one of his contacts. Thank goodness we were able to buy some extra food and treats for the children, because number two son has given Kin a good talking to after his last visit. Number Two Son was quite upset about the whole situation when he saw how Kin spent his days lazing around while I struggled with the finances. Well guess what? That contract job has ended and now Kin is jobless again. Number Two Son has come to the rescue once more and he told me yesterday that one of the cousins has offered to give Kin another job."

"Wonderful! Things seem to be getting better for you. There is more, isn't there? I feel it in my……..," chuckling at her own joke, Lowe gestured to her friend to continue.

"Well, the cousin lives on Java, the main island. They are talking of moving way out on the eastern coast of the island now. They asked me to look after the older ones until they are settled and then they promised Second Son that they would send for the rest of the family. What will happen to Ayin?"

"Don't worry old friend. Remember what the Goddesses told you? This is a time of separation for Ayin, the time for her to feel the energy of the first abandonment."

"You mean Lian will leave Ayin behind!? She is barely two years old, a baby who still needs her mother even one who keeps rejecting her!"

"It is what we hoped for, isn't it? For Ayin to stay with you so that you can teach her in peace. The first five years of a child are so important, Old One. These are the years where she will absorb the teachings and collect all the tools that you and I can give her. Even though she will not remember them until her later years when they will float to the surface of her consciousness as needed, they will never be forgotten once imprinted. Let's take it in a positive manner my friend, be at peace with it and prepare to enjoy every precious moment with your granddaughter."

Time marched on and the village of Sungai was as sleepy and quiet as it had been since the war ended. Although the government had changed hands and the whole country was now liberated from Dutch colonial rule, it did not seem to affect the villagers, for the community continued with their daily routines the same way as they did before the war. Both communities, those of Chinese heritage and of native birth, were co-existing peacefully, blissfully unaware of the rising unrest looming on the far horizon across the ocean.

At the same time, the Liu family was having a much-needed peaceful existence together since the departure of Lian and her husband. The old friends continued to meet on a regular basis, exchanging news and the local gossip as they kept a watchful eye on their active charges.

It was Lowe's turn to visit her friend again this time and Apho happily opened the door to welcome her in. "Come in Lowe, come in! I am so glad that you have to do the walking this time! It is unusually hot today."

"Ah, when is it not hot in this country Old friend, besides you have the best cookies in the neighborhood," The midwife chuckled as she lowered herself gratefully into one of the rattan chairs. "Where is the Little One?"

"Where else? Look outside she is in the garden again! I have never seen a child who loves the garden so much. Just look at her! She is constantly talking to the trees and bushes, or is she? " With that sudden thought, the proud grandmother turned and raised her eyebrows, questioning her friend.

The wise Dukun grinned, "I wondered how long it would take you to notice that. Look closely, Wise One and listen. You will notice that this child is surrounded by the Devas of the nature kingdoms besides being surrounded by her guardian angels. There is a whole entourage surrounding this child at all times. Have you taken her to the ocean yet? She is also very connected to that kingdom, although it will take her a while to overcome the obstacles that need to be cleared in this area. Water, as you know, is a highly spiritual element and it will give her the peace she will need. I also see that the fact that her parents have left did not affect her at all, did it?"

"No, not at all. She has adjusted to the change very quickly. She did not ask or cry after her parents' departure. You were so right! Lian refused to take her and instead took the older Luan and of course, baby Suni. I finally heard from Lian. They have settled in Surabaya, far away on the East coast, as I told you before. They bought a house and so far, Kin is behaving himself in his job. I keep my fingers crossed though and hope that it will last and that the cousin will tolerate his arrogant behavior."

"As to your other question, yes I have taken her to the ocean and she loved it, but seemed to be afraid of the waves. Now that you have given me a bit more clarity on the subject, I understand her fear. It is almost a love-hate relationship she has with the water, isn't it? Or maybe it is the salt water getting into her eyes. She loves walking on the beach though and enjoys hunting for the small edible clams in the sand. It is amazing to watch her! She seems to blend so well with nature all around her whether it's the forest or the wide-open beaches. Watching her, I am a bit worried that Ayin thinks I am her mother, although she calls me Pho-Pho. She seems to have completely forgotten her own mother."

"I told you that she will be hit hard with both lessons of abandonment and rejection at a later age, when she finally understands what her mother has done. However, you are providing the necessary positive imprints right now, so that she will have the tools when she needs them and oh, will she ever need them! Emphasizing her connection to Mother Nature is the best thing you could do for her right now. During the times in her life which will be full of turmoil, she will discover that she can find solace in the woods and the tranquil energies of water."

Liamay interrupted the exchange between the two women, by bringing a tray with hot tea and cookies. Everyone who lived in a tropical atmosphere knew that a warm drink was the only solution to a hot and humid day. A cold drink would only make one feel the heat even more. A healer's household especially knew these special tricks to keep one's body temperature at an even rate.

Lowe appreciated the special cooling herbs that she could taste in the tea. "Apho sure knows her herbs," she thought, as she took a grateful sip from her cup. "Hmm jasmine and ginger in this one I think." Lowe looked questioningly at her friend.

"Your guess is almost correct, it is jasmine, hibiscus and a touch of mint to cool us off."

"I must savor the brew a lot longer next time to identify your secret mix."

They both enjoyed this guessing game and both would put great effort into concocting new tea blends for the other one to guess. So far Apho was in the lead!

"Just leave my cup on the table" Apho told her daughter. "I am going to see what the Little One is up to and bring her here for her snack as well."

"Good idea! I'd like to see her," the old dukun said with a smile.

Lowe watched her friend walk down the steps into the garden, then turned to face the elder daughter. "It's time to have that talk with this one," Lowe thought with an internal sigh. "How are you doing Liamay? Come and sit with me for a minute."

"Fine, Auntie. I think that mother and I are happy to have some peace and quiet around the house for a change. Did mother tell you that I have been offered a business opportunity in Singa?"

"Congratulations! When are you going? Your mother will miss you very much and I am sure that you know this already. I know that she has hoped that perhaps now that your sister and her family are gone, that you would try to make a life of your own here in the village. I did tell her that it was better for you to leave, but did not tell her why. I know how bitter and difficult things have been for you Liamay! " Lowe looked over the rim of her cup and sent waves of deep compassion to the young woman sitting before her.

Startled, Liamay turned and glared at the healer. "Aiiyah! You know, you know, don't you? I should know by now that you can see these things!" Liamay gasped as she faced the compassionate gaze of the old healer.

"Yes, I know how your hatred burns within you. It did not happen, did it child? He was not successful in the end. Let it go, release it or that emotion of hate will fester like a wound and cause you much harm in the end."

Silent tears seeped out of Liamay's eyes as she looked helplessly at Lowe.

"How could he Auntie! He is Lian's husband, my brother-in-law, and he tried to rape me!" Eyes full of pain and rage glared at her listener. I'll never forgive him! I hate him will my whole being! I asked Lian if I could adopt little Ayin, since she has trouble with the child and I do wish to have a daughter of my own. Lian was happy to oblige but he would not allow it. I think that he's being very spiteful! Here comes mother. Please Auntie, don't tell her. It will hurt her and I don't want that to happen. Mother has suffered enough already."

"Of course Liamay you should know better than to demand my silence on such a personal matter. I always consider things like this to be confidential and no one else's business but the players involved in the drama."

"I will be leaving as soon as my papers are ready. I am sorry that I have to leave mother with the three children, but Chauna and Chee are no trouble at all. They can practically look after themselves. Besides, Mother just dotes on Ayin and is happy to have her to herself. I guess you two will never tell me what this whole business with Ayin is all about will you?" asked Liamay with a puzzled look on her face.

Lowe just smiled and chuckled but did not rise to the bait.

"I am sure that your Mother will adjust to all the changes happening in her life right now. She is a very strong soul."

Chapter Seven

Ayin could barely contain her excitement that morning. It was her birthday and her grandmother promised to teach her how to make those famous coconut cookies. The preparations began last night. She was allowed to stay up and watch the proceedings. First, grandmother was showing Chauna how to grate the coconut meat and extract its milky juice. That was a hard job and she was glad that she was not asked to help with that, especially when Chauna complained that the sharp edges of the grater had skinned her fingers. Next, came the boiling of the sweet base, which was a mixture of the coconut milk and a lot of sweet dark palm sugar. She even managed to snatch a chunk and pop it quickly into her mouth before getting caught. That in itself was exciting! Unfortunately, she was sent to bed before she could see how the mixture looked when it was finished.

She quickly got out of bed herself this morning. Chauna did not even have to wake her up and help her to wash. After all, she was a big girl of 4 years of age, wasn't she? She could barely contain herself as she ran into the kitchen and looked around for the familiar dark brown mixing bowl. There it was, not far from the stove. Ayin stretched herself up on her toes, her nose touching the edge of the bowl as she peeked inside. She felt as if her whole tummy giggled with glee, as the wonderful aroma of sweet coconut wafted into her nose. Carefully she reached over with one finger and was about to dip that lucky finger into the thick syrup, when she was unceremoniously grabbed by the waist and lifted away from her prize.

"No, no Ayin! Stay away from that bowl child!" Apho shook her head as she lowered the little girl away from temptation.

"I just want to taste it, to see if it tastes good!" Ayin pleaded. "Please, Pho-Pho, one lick?"

"Maybe later after your breakfast and after we finish mixing the dough. Now come and eat your porridge."

Ayin could not spoon her porridge into her mouth fast enough that morning. Her eyes kept following her grandmother, as the old woman walked to and fro, carrying various ingredients from the cupboard to the kitchen table. Chauna and big brother Chee came in to join her for breakfast, as Ayin spooned her last mouthful and gulped everything down with some warm tea. She spilled drops of tea and bits of porridge on the table in her haste to swallow.

"She's doing it again, Pho-Pho!" Chauna told her grandmother after looking at her younger sister with disgust. "You'll get a tummy ache again if you keep eating like that!" Chauna frowned in disapproval at her messy sister.

Ayin ignored her sister and sat up on her knees to see what Grandma was up to next. "What are you putting in there Pho-Pho? Can I roll the dough too please? How come Chauna gets to help? Mmmm! It smells good already! Can I have a taste please, please?"

"Aiiyah! You are an inquisitive little monkey aren't you?" Grandmother chuckled. "All right now, let me see if you remember what I told you. What goes into the thick sweet coconut cream we cooked last night?"

"She does not know that Pho-Pho," Chauna said as she handed her grandmother a bowl full of eggs.

"Yes I do! Yes I do!" shouted Ayin. "Eggs go in first and then mix it and stir it! And then add lots of flour until it looks and feels like cookie dough! Can I break the eggs? Can I, Pho-Pho, please?" Ayin was moving her hands and arms excitedly in fast circles to show how she would mix the dough.

"I am a lot older than you little monkey and I am going to do it" Chauna announced as she pushed her little sister away from the mixing bowl.

Grandma smiled and said "Well, since she seemed to know the sequence Chauna. Why don't you show her and then let her break one egg into the bowl. After all, it is her birthday."

"Oh all right." Chauna compromised reluctantly.

"Me too!" yelled Chee, as he joined the group around the bowl.

"Why not", grandmother chuckled. Apho looked at her grandchildren's faces with deep gratitude. How she loved all of them. What a difference two years had made in these children's lives. They were so much happier these days, laughing a lot more, especially Chauna. She just loved playing the big sister role. She then thought of Chee and worried how one never knew what the boy was thinking. He seemed happy enough playing with the village boys and roaming the countryside wherever and whenever he felt like it. "He is growing so fast, what am I going to do with him?" she wondered.

Ayin's excited chatter brought Apho back to the cookie-making occasion. She took over the big wooden spoon from Chauna and proceeded to mix the eggs into the coconut mixture.

"Aunty Lowe is coming today, right? That's why we're making these yummy coconut cookies. I want to help! I want to help! They're my favorite cookies too! " Ayin tried to resist her sister's push and desperately clung on to the edge of the kitchen table.

"Bring her over here to this corner, Chauna, away from the bowl and let her play with this bit of dough." .

Chauna pried her protesting sister away from the bowl and took her to the opposite corner of the table. "Here, Pho-Pho says to make any shape you want. She will soon finish kneading the dough. We can all watch from here," Chauna said, as she noticed that Chee has joined them this morning. It was unusual for him to do that, as he would usually be gone right after breakfast to play with his friends outside. Grandma's cookies were very tempting!

Later that afternoon, two old friends were seated comfortably again under the shady leaves of the old mango tree and were enjoying the famous cookies with their tea. The old midwife chuckled as she recalled her encounter with Ayin earlier in the day. A whirlwind of an excited little girl almost knocked her over as she entered the hallway. A mop of black hair flying across a pink little face with big sparkling brown eyes rushed towards her, yelling at the top of her lungs. "You are here! Auntie is here! She is here!"

"She sure has grown hasn't she, Old One. What a bright one she is! Did you really teach her all about the fruits and vegetables you found at the market yesterday? She could name all the ones I had in the basket I brought."

"Not all of it. Sometimes I don't know where she gets her information from. I asked her once and she told me that Old Man told her. I don't know whom she is talking about. Do you know anything about this?"

"Sorry, my friend. That is strange however. She will usually tell you when I have taught her something."

"Yes, I have no trouble there at all. She is so happy every time she has spent some time with you. She tells me everything she has learned from you. By the way, thank you for the doll you brought her as her birthday gift. All she has are the ones I taught her how to make herself out of bits of cardboard and cloth. She is so creative and so nimble with her fingers at this age, but still, it is such a treat for her to get one that is store-bought."

"Don't mention it. It is my pleasure to do so. It warms my heart to see her so happy Old One. You are doing a great job raising her."

"You are doing your part too, remember. I am constantly amazed at what that child remembers. The curious thing is that she is genuinely interested in everything around her. She loves helping to cook and has begged me to buy her a little cooking pot. You should have seen her this morning, all covered in cookie dough! She even remembered the mixing sequence Lowe, how about that!" Apho shook her head with wonder and pride.

"When I gather my herbs, she always insists on coming along and is full of questions. Chauna never asks me any questions at all when she comes along, except to ask when we can go home."

"Well you certainly taught her well, because she picked the right fever herbs when she was with me a few weeks ago. Remember that patch by the front gate that I always miss somehow? Ayin kept going to it, telling me that she is picking 'fewfew' for you." Lowe chuckled.

The proud grandmother smiled and nodded her head at the compliment.

"I worry about the two older ones, Lowe," Apho continued to share her concerns with her friend. "Chauna was quite angry when her mother left. In the first few weeks she kept asking when she would be going to see her mother. Thank the Goddess that she seemed to have forgotten about it now. Chee never even bothered to ask where his parents were. Strangely, all three of them seemed to have forgotten that they have parents at all!"

"I tell you Old One, the Goddesses are putting things in place for these children. No use worrying about them. They have to live their lives just like all of us, with all the trials and the obstacles. It is out of our hands. We have only been given the task to help Ayin and that is what we need to do. Things will get more interesting as she grows older, my friend. I must ask my guides about the old man. I am very curious this is a new strand I have not seen before."

Chapter Eight

New Years day had come and gone. All the firecracker shells had been swept from the streets and the village slowly returned to its normal drowsy self. Chinese New Year had always been a joyous celebration and this year was no exception for the Liu family. They had enjoyed all of the excitement - especially Ayin, the youngest member and the one who was the most spoiled, according to her sister Chauna. Ayin was old enough to be able to understand all the preparations for the festivities and enthusiastically wanted to help everywhere. She was mostly underfoot in the kitchen and grandmother had quite a challenge keeping her from burning her little hands on the hot cooking stove.

Apho heaved a sigh of relief one warm afternoon when she spotted Lowe walking to the door.

"Well not only is it nice and cool here, but it is amazingly quiet for a change!" Lowe chuckled, as she handed her friend a basket of treats.

"Yes, they are finally asleep for their afternoon nap."

Something in Apho's voice caught Lowe's attention, but knowing her friend, she waited patiently and continued chatting about the weather until her teacup arrived. Apho picked up her own cup and settled herself down with a sigh. Looking up at her friend she said, "I suppose you know already, or have felt the change at least. I knew that you did as soon as I saw you outside my door. You were supposed to come tomorrow, but here you are today."

Lowe nodded her head silently and quietly encouraged her to continue. Her heart ached for this beloved friend. She knew this morning when she woke up, that the day both of them had dreaded had finally come. The Goddesses had sent her the dream message and it was not an easy one for her to accept, let alone for this doting grandmother.

"The letter came this morning." Apho quietly continued as a gentle rain of tears began to fall from her eyes. "I am to take the three children across the ocean and leave them with their parents. The tickets were in the envelope and I have only three days to pack. This is too soon!" Apho wailed.

With deep compassion, Lowe got up and gently gathered her friend into her arms, holding her, as Apho sobbed against her shoulders.

"Tell me what happened." she said gently, as she handed Apho a handkerchief to wipe her nose and tears. In getting her to tell the story, she hoped that it would ease the pain somewhat.

"I did tell you that my second son came to visit during the New Year's celebration?" Apho resumed her story, as she dabbed at her eyes. "My husband, his father, chose him to be the head of the family before he died. You know that my oldest son is just like his father, a very gentle man who does not have the ability to look after the family. That is why Second Son had to take over and he has done such an excellent job all these years looking after me and all nine of his brothers and sisters as well. Lian had always been his favorite little sister and she was almost like his daughter in a way, because she was only six years old when my husband died."

"Second Son was not happy when he came. He did not like how I had cared for the children. I had never sent Chauna and Chee to the village school, for I did not like the Chinese school and I did not like the Native school either. The Dutch school where all my children were educated was gone of course, and so I kept them home. They were all very happy, where is the harm in that? He asked why I had not taken them to Lian. I told him that Lian had asked me to keep them a bit longer because she got pregnant again and could not handle six children on her own. If she keeps getting pregnant like this, Lowe, what is to become of these children? You know that she is like a child herself!"

"Don't get yourself sick over all of this, dear Sister. Trust me, this will be her last babe and it will be the son she has asked for all these years."

Apho sighed, "Second Son said that Lian and Kin have to take responsibility for their own children and that I am to drop them off and leave immediately. He was the one who bought the tickets and would not budge from his decision. My poor Ayin!" Apho burst into tears again.

"The Goddess did say five years." Lowe whispered as tears gathered in her own eyes too.

Another sunny day, another blue sky and yet, the lonely figure seen walking along the path did not seem to be aware of nature's beauty. Not even the brilliant hibiscus blossoms could tempt a smile from this traveler that day. Head bowed, her shoulders slightly bent as if she carried a heavy burden, the old woman steadily made her way to a gate at the side of the road. As she pushed the creaking gate open, the front door of the cottage before her opened at the same time.

"What took you so long?" Lowe greeted her friend with a tease to get a smile out of her. Apho smiled tiredly as she handed her friend a basket.

"I wanted to pick the jackfruit from the garden to bring to you. It has finally ripened. It was one of her favorite fruits you know!"

"Aiiyah! I know Dear One. She liked all the fruits in your garden. Everyone knows how wonderful your mini orchard is. You have at least one tree each of half a dozen fruit varieties. Come, I have created a new blend of tea ready just for you and made my special cookies as well. They might not be as good as yours but they are quite tasty and my grandchildren like them too. Then you can tell me all about the difficult journey you have been on."

"Mmmm! What did you put in this tea, Lowe? Let me see, I can taste chrysanthemum blossoms, orange peel and mace?"

"Ahah," Lowe shouted with glee. "Wrong guess, finally I could fool your taste buds this time old friend! It's not mace but a touch of Dong Quai."

"Dong Quai! At our age we don't need hormones any more!" Apho chuckled, grateful for the light banter.

"Oh yes we do we're still in female bodies! And speaking of bodies, how are you feeling my friend, are you well? That was a most difficult journey for you."

I am all right Old friend. My heart is broken, but I am all right. Don't worry too much about me. The Goddess will look after me, remember?"

Lowe shook her head as she noticed how drawn Apho's face was. It must have been a horrendous trip. Traces of deep pain still lingered in those dark brown eyes. Compassionate thoughts flowed in soothing waves from her heart and she called in the healing channels of the Goddesses to help this dear Soul.

After a few sips of the herbal mixture, Apho looked up at her friend and gave her a watery smile. "Thank you Old Witch, you know just how to brew a good cup and for some reason this is the right blend for us today."

"Coming from you that is a big compliment and I accept it gratefully."

"Well, I might as well tell you the whole sad story." Apho squared her shoulders in resignation. "The children were very good on the trip. Ayin was very excited at first, as there is just no fear in that child. She has never been outside our village and yet she wanted to see all the new things on the trip. Chauna and Chee were more frightened and both kept asking me where we were going.

I told all three the truth, which was that they were going to live with their real parents. Chauna apparently has some memory of her mother and became very quiet. Chee was at first excited to meet his father and wanted to know if his father was going to take him places and play games with him. I hated to tell him the truth, so I kept quiet and let him hold on to his dreams for awhile."

"What about Ayin, our little one?"

"Aiiyah! She had no idea. She did not understand the meaning of the word Mother. I always did say to you that she thought of me as her mother, even though she called me Pho-Pho. It was heart wrenching Lowe. Ayin clung to me when we got to the house. She would not have anything to do with Lian even after she began to understand what Mammy meant. That's what Lian insisted the children call her and to call Kin, Pappy, using the Dutch words for Mummy and Daddy. We finally had to drug Ayin to sleep before I could leave. Aiiyah! My heart broke when I left!" Apho lamented quietly as she sobbed in her handkerchief.

Lowe insisted that her friend sip more of the restorative tea before she encouraged her to continue.

"I just received Lian's first letter. I made her promise to write me right away and as frequently as possible. It was not a good household, as you can well guess. Kin had another quarrel with the cousin and you and I more or less knew that that would happen. Kin, as usual, walked away from the job in a huff.

They were able to hire one of the villagers as a maid to help with the children and apparently Second Son had sent some money to help out.

Our poor Ayin was apparently beside herself. The trauma that child had to go through by being suddenly transplanted from my arms to a house of chaos!

Lian wrote that Ayin screamed for days and, not only that, she ran away the next day after I left. Can you imagine that! A five year old running away from a strange home in unfamiliar surroundings! There were paved streets everywhere, big strange houses all around the neighborhood and yet this child ran away! Not once, but every time they left her alone! Lian was so disgusted. Here, read it yourself." Apho handed Lowe a stack of papers that were well-worn from having been read so often

Lowe shook her head sadly, as she read the tale of woe:

"What did I do to deserve this child from hell? I am the laughing stock of the neighborhood! No one has ever heard of a five-year old running away from home! I had to have the maid constantly running after her. I hired the maid to help with the cooking and cleaning and instead I had to assign her to keep a constant eye on Ayin. We cannot afford to hire another one! What have you done to her Mother? You have spoiled her rotten, and now I just don't know what to do with her any more!

On top of everything else, Chee has been another handful of trouble. That boy would not listen to Kin his own father! Kin told him that he had to ask permission every time he wanted to go out and that he had to go to school every day. What did this ungrateful boy do, but run away as well. We had our hands full running after two very spoiled children. Kin of course had to take the broom to Chee but strangely, would not touch Ayin. I had to spank that one repeatedly myself. She just cries and cries! All that spanking did not seem to help one bit! On top of everything else, she developed a bad case of stomach problems. She continually screams and doubles up with stomach cramps. Then we had to deal with diarrhea. I have never heard of a five year old with a stomach ache this bad!"

"Aiiyah!" Lowe groaned as she put the letters on the table before her. "Come with me." She told her friend as she headed towards the garden. "Let's do something about this."

"What do you have in mind?" Apho asked as she followed the Healer out into the garden.

Both women ended up before the altar in the shady part of the garden. It looked so different in the daylight, Apho thought as she stood beside her friend.

Lowe must have known that they would end up here for the altar seemed to have been prepared for a specific ceremony. Bright red, pink, blue and white flowers formed a colorful circle on the stone altar. Inside this fragrant circle, Apho recognized the five crystals used in another ceremony five years ago. It seemed only yesterday that they were both standing in the same spot in the moonlight.

Both elders bowed reverently towards the altar to show their intent. Lowe moved forward and lit the joss sticks on the altar. Immediately, fragrant tendrils of bluish smoke curled lazily upward into the air above. The gentle puffs floated in between the shifting shadow patterns created by the swaying leaves of a nearby tree.

As Lowe began to chant, she handed three joss sticks over to her friend and kept three for herself leaving another three on the altar. The two friends began the ancient ceremony by bowing three times turning gracefully as they honored the four directions of the East, North, South and West. They moved the joss sticks up and down with each bow, as they called upon the Goddess to grant them a hearing. In a soft melodious tone, Lowe, as the shaman, voiced her request and sent it into the ethers with the ceremonial smoke.

Apho followed her friend's lead and chanted along. Maybe it was just her imagination or maybe the glare of the afternoon sun, but she thought that she saw a glimmer of light twinkling within each of the five crystal stones.

It felt as if they stood outside of time, as the stillness enveloped both elders. Lowe had her eyes closed as soon as she started chanting and bowing and then stood very still, barely breathing as the joss sticks in their hands continued to emit the sweet smoke. Apho breathed deeply and felt an immense sense of peace and well-being within her. She would gladly stay there forever if she could continue to bask in this cloud of blissful existence. She was gently brought back to the present, when she heard Lowe begin the thanksgiving closing chant.

Quietly, the friends walked back to the house and refilled their cups of tea.

"All right, Old Witch, what did the Goddess tell you?" Apho prompted.

"Aiiyah! First she said for us not to worry and then she showed me what would be in store for Ayin. The Goddess must have a strange sense of humor for she insisted that Ayin would be looked after. She has now passed the first transplant and has turned the corner. She will not remember much of her first five years until later in life, when the memories will be returned to her.

Everything will change for her as she enters a four year period of growth before the next transplant will occur again. Everything that will happen to her, is preparing her for the special job that she is born for. A handmaiden of the Goddess must learn all about human behavior, human suffering and human emotions. By experiencing each one, she will gain the wisdom to help the ones who will seek her."

"My poor baby! How can we help her?"

"Just with our prayers, my friend, just with our prayers. Shielding her from the pain of human suffering will prevent her from understanding a human life. She is like a rough diamond now, which needs to go through the process of cutting and buffing to become the brilliant blue diamond that she truly is."

"Remember the Moon Goddess at her birth? They finally told me who this granddaughter of yours really is, Old Friend. She comes from the realms of the Blue Ray; the Goddesses of the Blue Light, which include the Moon Goddess and the Goddess of the Oceans, and they will always protect her. Our beloved Quan Yin, whose divine Light shines over her is also part of the Blue Flame. She was chosen to represent a team of Goddesses who are being put in place, because of a big potential change in the world when you and I are gone. It is very big, Old Friend and I am already in awe of the tiny amount of information that they have shown me. It is not about us any longer. It is about the whole Universe itself. Just think! Our little Ayin has been chosen to be a part of this, if this potential change comes into play many years from now!

They also told me who the old man was. Remember the one Ayin told us about? He is the spirit of an old monk who is a Master in the knowledge of herbs and is part of the entourage of her spirit guides. He is the one who has been teaching and guiding her and will continue to be with her for a while, to help her understand the nature of the healing herbs. Many people will need good healers when this tremendous time of change is upon the World and Ayin is being groomed to become one of the teachers who can help a great deal."

"What happens if this potential does not occur? Apho blurted out as she listened in amazement.

"Ayin will then join us in the spirit world, Dear One and she will then return to her sisters, the Goddesses, who chose her in the first place."

The two old friends resumed sipping their tea, as they both tried to absorb the strange message. Both were uneasy with it and did not want to let the other one know how difficult it was to understand these concepts that the Goddesses had shared with them. They had faith that the Goddess would take care of everything and that thought was enough for both of them at the moment.

Chapter Nine

Two years later as the wheels of time continued their unending rotation, a familiar scenario rolled across the earthly screen in the form of a small female figure trudging along a muddy road. The monsoon season was on its final sweep and the rains had finally abated leaving the inevitable thick puddles of mud in every pothole to be found on this quiet stretch. The old woman dressed in her dark brown sarong carefully picked her way between the puddles as she breasted a small bundle of cloth against her modest kebaya. The kebaya was the traditional blouse worn by every woman in the village. Soon she reached her destination and pushed open a small wooden gate that had seen better days. Most of the paint had peeled away leaving patches of green here and there as a reminder of its former glory as a shiny green gate. The rusty hinges creaked in protest as they gave way to the force of an aged brown hand and the gate swung inward.

"Anybody home?" Apho called out as she knocked on the front door. Instantly the door was thrown wide open.

Spreading her arms wide Lowe exclaimed with joy, "Old One you are home! When did you get back? I knew that you were on your way home but was not sure when you'd feel like coming over. As a matter of fact I was planning to walk over to your house tomorrow to see if you were safely back. Come in. I have been thinking about you every day since you left, praying that all would be well for you."

Apho smiled at her friend's happy welcome. How she had missed this quiet place and how she missed their regular tea-time chats.

"I brought you a small gift from the big island Old Witch," she said as she handed Lowe the small cloth bundle.

"Aiiyah, you shouldn't have," Lowe eagerly unwrapped the bundle. "Aiiyah, thank you so much," she exclaimed in surprise as she picked up the small delicate white statue. "It is gorgeous, how beautifully the Goddess is represented! Where did you find one made of such fine white porcelain?"

"In the big city of course. Now how about a cup of tea and some of your cookies? I have not had time to bake any after my journey. You know that I took everything I baked for the children. I came home yesterday afternoon and was busy unpacking or I would have come earlier. There is so much to tell you about my first visit to see Ayin."

"Well go on, get started while I put the kettle on."

"She has grown so much Lowe. Two years since I left her. She is now seven years old and you were right. She does not remember our times here on the island and I am sorry to tell you that she does not remember you at all. She barely remembered me." Apho brushed her eyes sadly as she recalled her first encounter with a seven year old Ayin."

"Lian had told her that Pho-Pho was coming and she hugged me as soon as she met me but it felt so different. It was as if I was holding a stranger's grandchild. Mind you she must have felt something because as the days went by she would come and sit with me with a puzzled look in her eyes. I was quite honest with her and told her that she had lived with me for awhile. She kept asking me to tell her over and over again about our island home as if she was trying to remember.

Lian has changed all the children's names because of the Dutch school that she is sending them to. Second Son is still helping them financially and that is why she is able to send the children there. Kin is still having problems getting along at work. He is working for someone else now. He cannot accept orders from his boss and wants to have everyone follow his orders instead. Aiiyah! I really don't know how long that will last.

Lian told me that the Dutch people don't know our language and our names and so they asked her to change them to make things easier with the school registration. Ayin is now called Jena, Chauna is known as Joan and Chee answers to Charlie. I did not like the new names so I kept calling her Ayin and she liked it so much that she insisted the whole family call her, Ayin." Apho chuckled at the memory. "She has grown into a very strong willed young lady. Our baby has fire in her and is learning to stand up for her own rights."

"Names are powerful," Lowe interrupted her friend's story quietly. By giving her that new name, the Goddesses have truly hidden her now, as they said that they would. She is like a seedling, transplanted into a different flower pot and now needs to adjust to her new environment and grow into a new plant."

Apho nodded her agreement and continued her story. " Lian is still frustrated with her but has finally just accepted the fact that Jena is different than her siblings. As far as Lian was concerned she remains the strange unpredictable child whom nobody understands. One day I saw how she supervised her mother cutting a banana in two pieces. Jena insisted that Lian measure the banana with a ruler before making the cut! Her sense of fairness was very strong and no matter what Lian said, this child would not back down! You should have seen Lian's expression at this demand!" Both ladies chuckled as they both visualized this humorous scene.

"Lian told me later that this happens all the time. Jena will insist on everything being fair and will get very upset when she notices her mother handing over special favors to her sister Luan. You and I know of course that Luan is and always will be Lian's favorite child. She is a pretty girl and that is of extreme importance in Lian's mind."

"Luan is providing her with the challenges of sibling rivalry my friend. Ayin needs to feel and understand this, as painful as it is, because this emotion is so prevalent in every family."

"She must be receiving some kind of guidance then. I was surprised to see that a child at that young age continues to be very forgiving towards everyone in the family especially her mother."

"I told you that she is overlit by the Goddess of compassion herself. Negative emotions such as revenge or sibling rivalry are very thin within Jena's emotional field. This is one of the reasons that caused her to be very puzzled and frustrated. She does not realize that others have heavier emotions that are sometimes targeted towards her to help her understand the darker side of human nature."

"Jena has a little friend now, a girl her age who lives just across the street. Both of them go to the same school and they seemed to get along very well."

Both ladies chuckled again when Apho told her how Jena continues to upset the family's routine with her unusual behavior.

"How is Liamay doing? With all the news about Ayin, I have not had a chance to ask you about her."

"She is doing quite well in Singa. She has her own business now, a cottage industry really, in her own home. She makes mungbean flour and sells it to the stores in Malay. Besides that she also runs a small bakery. She sends me a message through one of the cousins telling me that she is planning to visit Lian. I think that she is still hoping that Kin will agree to give Ayin up for adoption.

Liamay definitely needs help that only a female child could provide. Right now after I have seen Ayin, I don't think she's the right one for Liamay. What do you see Old Witch?"

"I agree with you. The Goddess has other plans for Ayin. That child is too smart, although she likes the art of cooking she is not suitable to work in a bakery. Besides Liamay will never understand Ayin and would find that out soon enough."

Part Two

<u>The Seedling</u>

The seedling was firmly rooted in a bed of rock and mud
The emerging tender stalk felt secure with that connection
And it grew daily exploring its new environment
Pushing its new growth further upwards towards a new destination
The seedling did not know where that was
But instinctively felt the directional pull upwards
It experienced many hazards on its journey
It had to face currents that pushed and pulled it to and fro,
It had to deal with falling debris that would hit its tender skin
Other swaying plants in the water would lash out at its vulnerable tip
Then there were painful nibbles of various creatures to deflect
And yet nothing deterred the seedling from its purpose
Bravely it continued to raise its growing tip
One more inch.
Day by day

Chapter One

"Jena, Jena, Auntie Liamay is coming", Suni was jumping up and down as she relayed the exciting news to her sister.

"When, when is she coming?" Jena could barely contain her excitement. Pho-Pho had told her how Auntie Liamay had helped raise her in the village when mother and father left. However no matter how hard she tried, Jena could not remember how Auntie looked. Jena was somewhat disturbed about this because she felt that besides Pho-Pho, Auntie Liamay was the one who took care of her as a baby. How awful it would be if Jena could not even recognize her if she met her own aunt on the street! And now the promised visit had come to fruition.

Everyone was just as excited when Auntie finally arrived. Jena could not stop looking at her aunt and thought how beautiful she was in her native sarong and kebaya outfit. She had only seen her grandmother and some of the native ladies wear the traditional dress on a daily basis. Jena thought that the outfit was beautiful and secretly day-dreamt that one day she would wear the beautiful colorful lacy kebaya too. She asked Mother once why she never wore the batik sarong herself. Mother told her that it was not practical and that the western dress was much more comfortable and of course much more the in-thing to wear. Jena understood what that meant. Everything the ladies of the west wore was in fashion and all the women would strive to wear the same styles as much as they could reproduce on their sewing machines. The West was that vague foreign land where everything good and beautiful seemed to exist and the ladies in town would try to emulate anything to gain recognition in their circles.

"Don't you understand," mother would say, "The white people are more beautiful, and they are smarter than we are, and more educated. Look how beautiful their big blue eyes are, how straight their noses, how golden their hair and how white their skin. Now that is beautiful! Your cousin Greta is beautiful because her mother is half white."

Jena did not understand any of it but knew from experience not to argue with her mother or she would get another spanking if she did.

As soon as Auntie was settled, she called the children to her and the presents were unpacked. Jena was beside herself when Auntie gave her a beautiful doll. She never had a doll that was purchased from a store before, not that she remembered anyway. The smiling pink and white porcelain face was framed by curly blond hair and to top it off, it had big blue eyes. It was Jena's happiest moment, a moment to be savored - for it did not last very long!

Auntie Liamay only brought two dolls. "Just for the two youngest girls," she said because Auntie did not think that the older sisters should be playing with dolls any longer. She brought another doll for five year old Suni and it caused an uproar! This doll was the exact opposite of 'Goldie', Jena's doll. Suni's doll was completely black, with tight black curls, big brown eyes and a small button nose. Suni did not like her doll and refused to take it. Instead she went into a temper tantrum which was very unlike Suni.

Suni never screams when she cries, only whimpers and hides in corners or under the table. She would do this every time mother would punish Jena and would not stop the crying until mother would stop the punishment. Mother could not understand this behavior. And neither did anyone else in the household except that they all knew that Suni would and could make herself very sick if Mother did not stop spanking Jena. Jena was extremely grateful to Suni for this even though she did not understand why Suni would do such a thing. Suni's reaction to mother's violent outbursts had saved Jena many extra encounters with the broom!

"It is my doll," Jena cried desperately, clutching her new doll. "Auntie Liamay gave it to me." A steady stream of tears washed over Jena's anxious face.

"I want you to give it to Suni, now" Mammy ordered. "She is younger than you are besides you are getting too old to play with dolls any way."

"I am not, I am not," Jena sobbed. "I love my doll, and if I have a daughter of my own one day, she is going to have lots of dolls." It was no use. Her heart screamed at the injustice of it all. With a deep sigh Jena handed Goldie over to Suni and kept telling herself to remember the many times that Suni had saved her from painful encounters with the broom or mother's hand.

Auntie Liamay did come to Jena's defense however by pointing out that the doll was a gift to Jena. It did not help matters, for Lian insisted that the younger child should have the doll.

Jena surprised herself that she got over the whole episode very quickly and started to make her own little cut-out dolls to play with. And, in the end, Suni agreed to share the doll with all the sisters after she had the doll to herself for a few days. She had soon realized how Jena quietly went off by herself, refusing to play with her or anyone else.

Auntie Liamay did not stay very long and Jena noticed that it was not a happy visit. It would be a very long time before Jena would see her aunt again.

Far away in a quiet, sleepy little village two elders sat under an old mango tree sharing a fragrant cup of herbal tea. The conversation seemed to be focused around Apho's daughters and her grandchildren again.

"Liamay was very upset when she came back from visiting her sister," Apho told her friend. " She did ask Lian if she could adopt Jena again but Kin would not budge. Liamay felt that he did it just to spite her. For some reason Liamay has nurtured a profound feeling of hatred and disgust towards Kin. She never liked him but her dislike seemed to deepen

after the children were born. They never got along and I don't blame Liamay because I am often angry at Kin myself. What do you think happened there Old friend?"

Lowe listened quietly to her friend but did not respond to Apho's last question. Instead she rerouted the conversation back towards Jena's adventures.

"It is as it should be. The Goddess knows what is at stake here and has set all the parameters to ensure that she is getting all the experiences she needs in her human life. Yes even the doll incident will help prepare her for her future life. I am just sad that this incident will have a very long lasting traumatic effect on Suni." Lowe successfully diverted Apho's attention with this last statement.

"You meant Jena, not Suni?"

"Oh yes, I meant little Suni. This is not a big lesson for Jena, she is surrounded with the Goddess light of compassion and will be able to transform this small dark strand into light easily. It is a different matter for Little Suni. It will cause a major blockage in her life. This soul came in not only to help Jena but she chose a heavy assignment for her soul self. Her challenge will be to recognize who Jena is, acknowledge her and accept her help. Her feelings of guilt and unworthiness will be a major undertaking for this one."

"It is so hard to see these children suffer," Apho wiped her tears away as she sighed heavily." They are still so young!"

"It is not the children's fault Apho, they are adjusting to and learning from their caretakers. Many are very advanced old souls and are in human child bodies for only a short period of time. They need to learn again how to be a child and how to learn from their parents. Once they reach adulthood they

must take full responsibility for their own actions and cannot blame their parents any longer.

Parents on the other hand have the responsibility of teaching the child how to be a loving human. You and I know that this is not always the case because many parents have not yet reached the state of a conscious adult and are often unable to become the models that the child needs. Your daughter and her husband are a perfect example. They are not bad people they have just chosen not to reach the higher level of consciousness of an adult human in this lifetime. The children choose their parents for a reason. In the case of your grandchildren, they must be looking for specific soul lessons from Lian and Kin."

"*You have given me much clarity Lowe. Being a human is not an easy thing is it? Especially a human parent! I know that you and I have had our share of challenges and troubles as a parent and we have had help from the Goddess. Just imagine those who do not belief in the Divine!"*

Chapter Two

Jena sat up very straight and tried to be very still facing the front of the class, watching the teacher intently. She wanted to win the prize very badly that day. The teacher had dangled that beautiful box of colored pencils like a golden carrot before the students for days now. Today was the day that a winner would be chosen. Today the teacher would tally all the scores earned throughout the week. Jena was sure that she had a chance because she had tried so hard to pay attention and to be on her best behavior. She couldn't help it that her mind often wandered during class. Jena's quick mind understood the lesson and was soon bored. Thus she daydreamed a lot and often did not hear the teacher's question which of course meant that she usually had the wrong answer. Many times she tried to cover her inattention by making her answer into a joke which made the class laugh but unfortunately not the teacher.

The teacher's voice seemed to be coming from the bottom of a deep well as she announced the winner.

Mernie has won again! A feeling of disillusionment and sadness flooded Jena's heart. It took a lot of effort to control her tears and to bravely join in the congratulatory handshakes.

"Mernie does not even draw as well as I do and the teacher said that she liked my artwork. I could do so much more with a new set of colored pencils," Jena sighed inwardly at the disappointment.

"Don't worry, Jena," Hildi, her friend tried to console her. "I like your pictures. You are a good drawer. I could never draw like you do."

Hildi's loyal words helped to ease Jena's feelings and gave her the resolve to try harder next time.

Her attention was suddenly brought back by the teacher's announcement that there wouldl be another chance of winning another prize. This time the teacher was looking at the most creative ink-mop. Jena immediately sat up straight with excitement. She loved making ink-mops! After all she had lots of practice since hers was always very quickly dirty with ink stains and the teacher did not like the student's writing exercises marked with ink spots.

"They just don't understand," Jena thought. "Sometimes my fingers want to write so fast because I have so many stories in my head that the ink makes blotches on the paper. I have to keep wiping my pen on my ink-mop to take off the excess ink and that takes time. And I forget and, and, and....", Jena's mind gave a huge frustrated sigh.

Jena couldn't wait to get home that day so she could get started on the ink-mop project. Her friend Hildi wasn't too thrilled at first when Jena suggested that they head home right away instead of waiting for their older sisters. The younger grades were always dismissed at least an hour earlier and usually the two girls would just play in the schoolyard waiting for Luan and Jill, Hildi's older sister, to get out of class.

Jena insisted however and as usual Hildi agreed. "Jena has always so many interesting ideas," Hildi thought. It was always difficult to refuse because she could be so persuasive. "I just hope I don't get in trouble with my parents when I get home. Jena is so lucky nobody in her family ever wonders where she is and her mother never even bothers to ask whether she is home or not. Mother thinks that Jena's family is strange. Well Jena is my friend and I'll stick with her, strange or not."

The two girls set out happily on their way home after leaving a message for their older sisters. They were about a third of the way home when suddenly the usually blue, sunny sky turned gray. The wind began to pick up and instantly the gray clouds began to turn darker still. A sudden tropical storm was about to break over their heads.

"Jena I don't like this", Hildi whimpered.

"Let's hurry then." Jena looked up uneasily and grabbing Hildi's hand began to pull her along encouraging her to walk faster. The girls began to increase their pace and were walking at a half run when the first sound of thunder rolled across the sky. Black boiling clouds were now racing across the heavens. They emerged from the side street they were on and faced the biggest, widest and longest street that they had to cross. There was no traffic, not one bike, not one wandering soul out that afternoon. It was so still as if everyone knew that it was absolutely madness to be out on the street at that time. In this stillness before the storm, two frightened little figures hurried along running hand-in-hand about to cross the main road. It suddenly seemed as if the distance that they had to traverse was a vast sea of black sinister tarmac. They had walked this road every day and yet that afternoon it had changed into an unrecognizable frightening obstacle course.

The storm exploded as they started to cross the street. Brilliant blue and white lightning zigzagged from the eerie glowing sky followed by loud crashes of thunder. Jena began to run across as fast as she could while pulling her screaming friend beside her. A tropical rainstorm can be an awesome sight for anyone for the rain will pour down like a torrent of water that is dumped from the sky. In many areas it will usually cause a flash flood and this was the case that afternoon. The girls had to run through an instant river of fast moving water with a strong muddy current that was carrying all kinds of debris.

It caught them in mid-point and that was when both lost their shoes. Without pausing Jena let go of Hildi's hands and quickly grabbed the shoes. She thrust a pair into Hildi's free hand, held a pair in her own free hand and grabbed the sobbing and screaming Hildi with the other. Both were now running in bare feet, utterly soaked and shivering with cold.

The storm that came up so suddenly, stopped just as suddenly when they reached the other side of the street. They proceeded to run into the next side road that would take them home and Jena insisted that they stop and put their wet shoes back on. She knew the dangers of walking with bare feet on the road where pieces of glass and other harmful garbage were scattered by the flooding waters.

"I'll never listen to you again", Hildi cried as they continued their journey home. "My mother will be so angry with me!"

"Just tell her that it is my entire fault Hildi. I don't mind taking the blame. This way you won't get grounded. Nobody at my house will care anyway. I'll bet no one will even ask why I am so muddy and wet and if I am all right."

"I don't care, you have a weird family and I am never going to walk home alone with you again," Hildi tearfully yelled at her friend as she ran towards her home.

Sadly Jena watched her friend as she slowly made her way to her own home. The storm frightened her a little bit when it first started but thinking back on the adventure, Jena realized that she had enjoyed the whole episode. It was exhilarating. She felt almost one with the wind and the rain. Even the lightning did not really scare her and amazingly she realized that she somehow felt safe throughout the whole experience. She could not put her finger on it but it felt as if there was something or someone protecting her.

"Hildi is right", she thought, "I am really weird!"

As Jena expected, no one at home wondered at her wet, dirty and tattered state. Quickly and quietly she snuck in through the open hallway that connected the main living quarters to the kitchen and the bathroom.

She had a quick shower and dropped her dirty clothes in the laundry basket where the maid would be picking it up in the morning. They could only afford one maid from the village and she had to do all the cleaning, washing and most of the cooking as well for the whole family. Mammy seemed to be away frequently and Jena never knew where her mother spent her days.

It was therefore very interesting when Jena heard the murmur of strange voices and found her mother talking to a couple of Indo ladies in the front room. The front door opened directly into this room and the children were not allowed to play or use this room. It was kept neat strictly for company. They never had many visitors and it was always an exciting occurrence for Jena when they did have strangers coming to visit, especially Indo ladies from the white-man's church.

Jena knew that her teachers at school were all Indos as well. Indos were the offspring of mixed blood, descendants from the union of Dutch people and the native population. They were always considered very beautiful for they had the white skin, and sometimes they were even born with the admired blue eyes and blond hair. Many times Jena wished that she was an Indo, especially after listening to her mother's frequent lament of how ugly they all were except for Luan. Luan, according to mother, was the only beautiful girl child and the only one who would marry well, which meant marrying a very rich man and being happy ever after. It was the ultimate dream of all the adolescent girls in the Chinese Community. Jena however could never understand this reasoning and would often peek at herself in the mirror and wonder what it was that would make her so ugly in her mother's eyes. She quickly understood the necessity of a rich marriage after being told that she was poor and that was why there was often not enough food or nice things for the family.

She had learned about the Dutch church at school from her teachers but had never been to one and did not know what people did in this thing called Church. Apparently the ladies were Sunday school teachers and were recruiting students for their school. Jena did not know what a Sunday school was and what they would be doing there. Mammy said that they could all go and explained that they would get cookies, snacks and do craft projects there. Jena was all for it for she loved crafts and frequently wanted to learn everything all at once. She sometimes found that people around her were just doing things so slowly. Jena often wondered why they could not do things in a much more efficient and faster way!

Hildi's mother must have forgiven her, because to Jena's delight, Hildi was allowed to join Jena and her sisters.

Rain drops were drumming hypnotically on the small cottage's roof as the two friends sat quietly in Lowe's tea room. That is what the midwife named the small rectangular room in her house. It was the time of the monsoon rains again and no one in his right mind would try to walk in this tropical torrent.

Apho was happy that she made it to Lowe's door just in time before the heavy clouds released their wet load to the earth below. "I've asked Lian to continue to speak to our little Lotus in our native tongue and Lian tells me that she remembers. Isn't she a very smart girl?"

Her friend smiled indulgently, "Yes she is, she has to be, Old One. There is so much that she has to learn and absorb in her short human life. And this special soul will rise to every challenge. You and I will proudly watch from afar."

"I am sometimes worried what she is up to. Lian, her own mother, does not seem to monitor her whereabouts all that closely. When I asked her what Ayin had been up to, Lian said that she had no idea!"

"Stop worrying so much. Remember she is protected by the Goddess. Nothing will be allowed to harm her; she is being groomed for a much bigger job than the other girls her own age. Didn't you tell me that she is attending the Christian Sunday School program?"

"Yes, what do you think about that?"

"That is wonderful! They will teach her the knowledge she requires. She will learn about the Christian belief system and this is just an introductory lesson for her."

"I have never been comfortable with their teachings Lowe, are you sure about this? Will it cause her to forget the teachings of our ancestors and the Goddess?"

"She will not forget what you have taught her but as I told you before the knowledge of the Goddess will be dormant within her for awhile. She needs to know the Christian story Old One. She will be teaching the Christians and must know all about their belief system before she can get their attention."

"It is sometimes so difficult just to be still and watch, isn't it Old Friend? It is not easy to be the detached observer when it involves the people you love."

Chapter Three

It was the beginning of a very interesting interlude in Jena's life for she found out that there were many different Churches in the world. It was strange for her to realize that many people belief that the God they were praying to was the only right one and that everyone should follow their belief system or go to Hell. The strangest part was that the God everyone was talking about seemed to be the same one.

Jena had heard the neighbors talking about their religion and that they were members of another church called the Catholic Church. The Sunday school ladies who came to recruit them were members from another church called the Protestant Church. Jena found this all very strange because both churches seemed to worship someone named God. The same name so it must be the same person, Jena thought, but the two congregations did not like each other and would often not speak well of one another.

Being a curious young girl she dismissed these strange thoughts and instead focused on the exciting things that would happen on that first Sunday School Day. It was on a Sunday of course that the children were taken to the nearest Protestant church basement for the first class. Jena was immediately enthralled. She loved every thing that day and from then on would be the one who insisted that they attend Sunday school on a regular basis. Her sisters soon dropped out and refused to go any longer, but not Jena!

Like all the other children she loved the cookies and the treats but Jena was particularly mesmerized by the stories that the teachers were telling the children. Jena decided that this was so much better than an ink-mop project. It was fascinating to discover that there was something called Heaven where people go when they died. Then there was this very holy old man called God who lived there and who knew if you were bad or good and who would punish you when you were bad. Jena did not care whether it was true or not but she loved stories and was the only one who would beg the teachers to loan her some books so she could read more about this strange God Being. The people who believed in him and who prayed to him were all called Christians because God had a son who was called Jesus the Christ. Jena was upset when she first heard the story of the crucifixion. She did not think God was a very good father. The teachers told her that everyone should love and honor the Father God but Jena did not want to love a father who allowed his only son to be murdered like that. He was supposed to be God wasn't he? God was supposed to be a super being, a magical being who could do anything and who was in charge of everything in this world. According to the Bible, his son Jesus was able to perform all kinds of miracles like making more fish, bread, wine from water and even walking on water! Now why would a father have such a magical son crucified? Jena struggled with these concepts and finally decided that Mammy was right after all.

"Don't you believe in what they are telling you in that Sunday School Jena. That is all white people's religions and you are not white! We believe and pray to the ancestors and the Buddha, they are real! They say that they are Christians and that their God tells them to be good to other people but look what they are doing! We cannot go to the good beaches, it is all fenced in and it is only for the white people. Only the Whites and the Indos are allowed to go to the big fancy restaurants and clubs. Furthermore you cannot get a good job unless you speak their language. Why do you think your father and I are sending you to the White Man's School even though we can barely pay the tuition fees for all of you? No, don't you ever get sucked into that Christian religious nonsense!"

Jena was able to see with her own eyes what her mother was talking about one day. Uncle Khew came to visit with his car and took all the children for a ride. That was so much fun for all of them. They finally were able to see more of the city in which they were living. Uncle drove all the way to the beaches and Jena finally saw what a beach and an ocean looked like. They could only drive by and peek through the fence at the sunny beach and at all the white children playing in the sand. Most of the adults were either in the water or lying on the sand sunning themselves. Jenna found that a very strange habit because she was always told to stay out of the sun and to bring her umbrella with her during the hottest hours of the day. She could not understand why there was such a strange division among people just because of the color of their skin. She also realized and learned very quickly not to say anything about the matter because it got the big people so angry when they talked about it.

Jena could not remember walking on a beach or playing in the ocean waves although Pho-Pho told her that she had been taken to the beach when she was younger. Secretly though the rolling and crashing waves with their strange booming sound brought fearful emotions in Jena and she could not understand why that would be so. She was happy in a way that there was a fence surrounding the beach and that they could not go near the water. It was to be a love and hate relationship throughout her life.

Coming back to the new information of God, Jena kept wondering, "Who is this God anyway and where did he come from?" At least Jena knew who her ancestors were and that Buddha was a very holy person who lived a very long time ago and taught people how to be nice to each other. Jena liked that idea because she could never understand why people could be mean to each other. Just the idea to be mean felt uncomfortable like a shirt that was too tight and she was often bewildered when her sisters or her mother would accuse her of being mean. Her friends never accused her of being mean!

According to her mother, the Buddha is also a god and all the Chinese people pray to him. Chinese people do not go to churches, they go to temples or build their own altars. Mother would build a temporary altar in the garden during special times of the year and make all the children pray with fragrant joss sticks. Jena did not mind doing it and enjoyed the special celebrations because it always involved special foods that she loved.

Being a seven year old Jena did not delve too deeply into this puzzle of the different gods and continued to enjoy all the free Sunday school activities. Sunday school offered Jena the opportunity to experience many things that would not have been available to her. She and Hildi were the only ones who went on the road trip that took them to a wonderful inland pond for a swim and a church picnic for the day. It was an unusual treat for the girls.

Every time Jena found something that interested her, she would focus on the subject with her whole being enthusiastically and would engage anyone, who would listen, in a lively conversation. Mrs Bin, the next door neighbor was frequently subjected to Jena's narration of her exciting Sunday school adventures. Mrs. Bin's youngest son was teenage Jimmy who did not tell her any of his adventures. Therefore she was quite taken with this precocious and amusing child. During one of these encounters Mrs. Bin began to tell Jena about her church, the Catholic Church that is, and how much better it was. Jena was immediately intrigued and Mrs. Bin finally promised to take her to Mass the next Sunday morning. Mass, at the Catholic Church began at seven in the morning immediately after sunrise when the temperature was still nice and cool.

Lotus Child

Jena could not stop talking about the invitation. Before long the whole family was sick and tired of listening to her and she was told to be quiet. That was the reason that Jena overslept that Sunday morning because no one bothered to wake her up. Going to Mass in a Catholic church was just not an important thing as far as the family was concerned.

Not so for Jena, she was so distraught when she found out that Mrs. Bin had already left. Jena cried and cried as she huddled before the neighbor's door until Jimmy, Mrs. Bin's sixteen year old son took pity on her. Jimmy was always nice to her, sometimes taking her under his wing and offered to do so again. He told her that this was the only time he would bike her to Mass because he himself would have nothing to do with his own church. They both crept quietly into the pew where Mrs. Bin was already seated. They were not that late after all. The priest and the altar boys were just walking up the aisle towards the altar at the front of the Church.

Jena was fascinated and awed as she looked around her. This Church was definitely different than the one at Sunday school! The ornate, gilded pictures and statues placed along the sides combined with the large colorful stained-glass windows high on the wall created a feeling of magic. For an impressionable seven year old who had an insatiable thirst for knowledge and who was accused of having too much imagination, it was a fairytale realized.

Unfortunately it all came to an abrupt end and soon Jena was not allowed to go to any church any longer. "Why, but why can't I go any more?" Jena was truly distraught and disappointed. Her mother was quite firm on the matter. "I don't like what they are teaching you at that school. You are beginning to believe all those Christian stories and that is not right. Besides, Hildi's mother and I agree that both of you are far too young to go on your own to this Sunday school."

"But, but...." Jena started to argue.

"No, Jena," Her mother glared at her. "And don't you dare try to go on your own. Joan is to keep an eye on you. Furthermore you are not to bother Mrs. Bin any longer, did you hear me?"

That ended Jena's short Sunday school career and soon after that another unusual circumstance changed the flow of her life once again. A lively seven year old could not be expected to retain some of the teachings and without regular input Jena soon forgot all about the stories of a being called God.

"What is that all about Lowe?" Apho looked questioningly at her friend after she shared the updated news from her grandchild.

"It is all in perfect order Old One. Jena needs to learn all about God from a different angle. She needs to learn that people have created the different religions because of their different perceptions of who God truly is. She is still a child and this is only the beginning of all the lessons she has to absorb. She will understand soon that there is only one Creator humans call God that we all pray to here on Earth."

"I don't know about you but I have never understood this Christian god the various Missionaries are trying to convert us to."

"It is really the same God we pray to through the Goddess. Don't worry about it, we have the Goddess and that is enough for us to know. After all she knows who the Creator is, she is his Goddess, his messenger, and his angel who looks after us here on Earth. The creator has chosen many Goddesses and Masters to help us all and you and I have chosen to follow the Goddess Quan Yin. According to one of our ancient legends, Quan Yin was a virgin Princess who devoted her life to the Buddha. She achieved the state of enlightenment and was about to ascend into Heaven when she heard the people's prayers, especially the women. You know as well as I do how some babies are killed in China because they are girls and how some young brides are killed as well when they do not produce a baby right away."

"I am so glad that our ancestors left that country. I have never traveled back there myself but I do hear the heartbreaking stories from those who have gone back for a visit. Thank the ancestors that we can pray to the Lady of Compassion to help our poor sisters. Will this Christian message confuse her Lowe? Will it make her forget the Goddess even more?"

"It is not the time for her to meet our Goddess yet. She will meet and get to know the other Goddess first, the one who is called Mary, the Holy Mother. That is why Jena is being introduced to the different Christian churches at this point in her life. It is easier for a child to accept different belief systems than for us adults. Besides all the Goddesses work together and have full knowledge of everyone's journey.

Lotus Child

Mary and Quan Yin are both part of the Divine Feminine Creator energy. Both will have a major role to play in the Lotus Child's life in this lifetime.

Chapter Four

Uncle Khew dropped by again with his car one Saturday morning and to Jena's delight he offered to drive the children to the zoo and pick them up again at the end of the day. Jena had never been to a zoo and could barely contain her excitement. To her astonishment her brothers and sisters did not want to go at all. The whole excursion was about to be aborted and Jena was beside herself with the possibility of not being able to go and see the animals. She was not allowed to go by herself of course and so she cajoled, begged, whined and groveled until finally her big sister, Joan, agreed to go with her. Jena promised to be eternally grateful to her sister.

As far as Jena was concerned it was the most magical day ever. She could not stop talking about it. Big Sister had a different story to tell however when she was asked how the day went.

"It was not bad except that Jena kept making up ridiculous stories about animals coming up to her and talking to her."

"They did so", Jena insisted. "The donkey was following me and offered me a ride on his back."

"There was no donkey, you liar," Big Sister was disgusted. "See I told you she makes up these weird stories all the time!"

Not wanting to continue the argument, Jena turned and ran away to her special place in the garden amongst the banana trees. Away from accusing stares and pointing fingers Jena sat on her makeshift swing between two huge banana trees. With her feet she proceeded to rock herself gently to and fro, and huddled this way, she allowed the tears of misery to drip and streak down her cheeks. It was a good thing that her mother did not see her there because she had not dismantled the crude swing as her mother ordered her to do.

Jena had wanted a swing badly when she saw some children playing on one and had decided to make her own. She had tied a heavy rope between two banana trees in the garden and then rigged a flat board at the bottom of the loop. It was not a very stable swing but it worked if you sat very carefully on the board and kept your feet on the ground most of the time. Unfortunately Mother had found out about the swing and had angrily told her that she was damaging the trees. Banana trees have very soft trunks and the ropes were cutting into the outer layers of their trunks. She was told to take the swing down immediately. Jena promised to do so because she did not want to hurt the banana trees. However she was glad that she still had her sanctuary today.

"I am not going to cry in front of everybody or they'll make fun of me again. Why am I so different, why do

I see things that are not real?" Jena asked herself. "Why does my family hate me so? Why can't I be just like everyone else? Why do I sometimes hear things in my head? Am I going crazy?" Anguished questions were tumbling and turning in her head like a wheel that would not stop.

Then a gentle voice, "It is all right Jena. Close your eyes and breathe as if you are going to sleep and feel us with you." Jena did not know whose voice was in her head. Sometimes it sounded like her own voice but it always brought a deep calmness within her. It was not like seeing with your eyes, Jena decided, it was more like a feeling that there was someone there. Sometimes, if she sat very still in her quiet place in the garden, she could feel the loving presence of the beautiful lady of the voice. Jena did not know who she was, just accepted the presence the way she accepted her relationship with the animals and the trees around her. They were her friends and a very lonely little girl needed loving friends who did not call her names or accuse her of lying and being strange.

Fortunately the teasing, the name calling did not last too long this time as another major change descended upon the whole family. Jena was delighted when she found cousin Kosen was at the house when she came home from school a few days later. Jena loved her big cousin Kosen. He was such a gentle soul. He never made fun of her and never joined in the raw teasing of her siblings.

"Kosen, when did you get here? Are you staying longer this time? Please tell me another story?"

Kosen smiled and chuckled as he ruffled her hair. "The same Jena, always the one with the questions and the demand for stories. Are you behaving yourself this time?" He did not quite know why, but this little cousin tugged at his heartstrings and he could not ignore her questions.

Jena often wished that he was her big brother and that he would live with them. Little did she know that her wish was about to come true!

"Really, truly, is cousin Kosen going to live with us?" Jena could barely believe the news. How wonderful that Kosen would be in charge of the household. It did not matter to Jena that this was happening because her mother was about to leave her again. Jena knew that things were not right when she did not see her father coming home for weeks. Now her Mother was going away to the Big City where Pappy was now living apparently. Mammy was taking Johnnie the youngest one with her this time and she was leaving the rest of the brood behind with Kosen as guardian and babysitter.

Jena was very happy with the situation. Kosen had so many interesting stories: tales about ancient magic in that far away country called China, tales of legendary kungfu heroes who possessed strange powers, tales about monks from ancient temples who taught the arts of chi, the magical energy that could be used for powerful things. Jena could not get enough and would constantly insist on Kosen's attention.

For the first few weeks after Kosen moved in with the children he was appalled at what he discovered. He had not visited that often and when he did it was always for quick visits. He found out that the children did not know the rudimentary skills of proper table manners. Jena was the worst of the lot. She did not know how to use the proper utensils and was grabbing her food and gulping it down like a little monkey.

"No, no, Jena. Here, you hold the spoon in your right hand and use it to bring the food to your mouth. No you cannot grab the food with your left hand at the same time. That is a fork Jena and you use it this way."

"She always eats like that Kosen," Luan helpfully explained. "Mammy says that she was born under the monkey sign and that is why she behaves like one. She is always climbing trees and eating wild berries."

"I don't care. I wish I was a real monkey." Jena stuck her tongue out at her sister.

Over and over again, Kosen patiently sat with Jena helping her to understand that clawing at your food and stuffing it in your mouth was not good for the digestive system. He found out very quickly that Jena was indeed prone to frequent stomach aches. No one had paid any attention to what this little girl had been eating. At one point Kosen caught her stuffing herself with raw mango slices that had been marinated in hot chilly peppers. On another day he found her drinking the vinegary juice out of a jar of pickled cucumbers.

"Wash your hands again," Kosen reminded all the children constantly. "What has been happening here? He questioned sadly. "Hasn't your Mammy been teaching you how to behave at the dinner table?"

"Mammy is never home," Jena volunteered. "And Pappie never eats with us. Why do we have to learn all this funny stuff Kosen?"

"Because you are growing into adults and you will have to function in society. You have to know how to behave properly or you will never get a good job. You will meet many different people, Jena, and they will laugh and make fun of you if you don't know how to behave properly." Kosen tried to instill the basic social skills he had learned himself when he grew up and realized how important it was to be able to be accepted in many social circles.

"I don't understand." Jenna complained. "Mammy never makes us wash our hands so often and I don't know how to brush my teeth."

Because she loved her cousin deeply Jena complied readily with his gentle and patient guidance except when it came to afternoon naps. No matter how many times Kosen peeked into the bedroom to make sure that the children were all asleep, Jena somehow managed to slip out the door time after time.

"I can't sleep Kosen," Jena defended herself when he reprimanded her. "There are so many interesting things to do outside."

"Where did you go? It is not safe for a little girl to roam around alone Jena."

"I am always safe Kosen, really the nice lady says so"

"Who is this lady, why have I not seen her? What stranger have you been talking to?" Kosen was slightly alarmed at this news.

"Oh, you can't see her, I am the only one who can and she always talks to me"

"Don't listen to her Kosen, she is making up stories again," Joan interrupted.

"I am not making up stories!" Jena yelled back

"It's fine Joan," Kosen calmly told the oldest one, "Go do your homework and I will look after her. Tell me more about the lady Jena and where on earth do you go every time you give me the slip?"

Jenna giggled, "The lady is an angel silly, you know just like the angels in your stories and she says that I am the only one who can see her. She is very beautiful Kosen, I like her blue dress and she says that one day I can have a pretty dress just like hers. She and I go to the railway tracks at the end of the street and we look for sweet berries and ladybugs. I wanted to catch some and put them in a jar but the lady says that it will make the ladybugs cry, so I didn't do it."

Kosen did not know what to make of it all and decided to let the child enjoy her own imaginative creations. After all there was not much happiness for this peculiar child somehow and Kosen could not understand why his aunt has rejected this fourth child.

Then there was the incident with the bikes. There were only two bikes for the whole family to share. Charlie of course being the oldest boy was allotted one and immediately claimed it as his personal property. The girls did not argue with him and agreed to share the second bike. Joan and Luan were the only two who were big enough to ride it which in Jena's opinion was not fair and she decided to do something about it.

Kosen had to face a very angry Joan one day when he came home from work.

"Kosen, look at my bike. It is all scratched and one of the pedals is crooked and bent!"

"Did you have an accident Joan" Kosen was puzzled for he knew how careful Joan was. She took her role as older sister seriously and considered herself in charge of the household.

"I didn't do it. It's Jena!"

"Jena? What did she do now?"

"You talk to her." And Joan dragged a very reluctant girl forward. Kosen sighed when he saw a very rumpled little urchin, with numerous scratches on her arms and legs glaring at him defiantly.

"I want to ride the bike too, Kosen, and I can do it you know, I really can!

I can show you"

"How can I get angry with this child?" Kosen said to himself. "She is so inventive and always initiates her own activities. She is taking control of her own development without even knowing it."

"You should have asked Joan and myself first Jena," Kosen tried to make her understand that she was still a minor in this household and should be monitored.

"You owe Joan an apology because she is your older sister and you need to respect her position".

Jena hung her head, "I am sorry Joan. I did ask you to teach me."

"You are too little Jena, you cannot even reach the saddle, your legs are not long enough." Joan answered in exasperation.

"I can still pedal, I don't have to sit on the saddle!"

"From now on, you must ask Joan for permission to use the bike Jena. And you are not to ride it on the street until you grow longer legs."

With a disappointed sigh, Jena quietly nodded her agreement and took herself out of the room back into the garden.

Back on the Island under the old familiar mango tree, the two friends were back at their favorite time of day, a time for a quiet chat with teacup in hand.

"I am so glad that my grandson, Kosen happened to live in the same city. He is one of my favorites. He is always respectful and loving towards myself and all his elders. He is just what Jena needs right now. When I found out that he was to look after the family I asked him to write to me and to tell me how the children are doing. I think he knows that Jena is of special interest to me. He did ask me, why Lian is treating Jena differently from the other daughters."

"What did you tell him?"

"Not much, just that she is a very special child, different from the others. Amazingly he agreed with me. I knew that I liked that grandson," Apho chuckled.

"You are right Apho, he is exactly the teacher that Jena needs at this point in her life. Remember what the Goddess told us, many teachers are being prepared for this child. Kosen is one of many and I am very sorry to tell you dear

friend that this gentle soul will go home not long after you do."

"No Lowe, why, why are they taking him home? He is still so young and has a whole lifetime ahead of him to enjoy."

"It is not for us to question the Spirits Old One. He was born specifically to help Jena in this lifetime. Once his mission is completed he will be rewarded with a family of his own for a few years before leaving this earth plane. He is the only one she will listen to right now. She does need to learn all the social skills in accordance with the rules of our human civilization. You and I know that she will live among many different people from many different cultures and needs to fit in socially. She will cross more than one ocean and live on the big continents of this world where she has to mingle with different cultures and adapt to different social structures."

Chapter Five

Jena responded well to Kosen's patient and gentle coaching. It was a happy time for Jena and she tried her very best to make her cousin proud of her. Every time she did something right, Kosen would reward her with one of his stories of ancient Chinese tales and legends. They continued to be Jena's favorites and apparently they were Kosen's as well. He was a scholar and, not only did he study the ancient myths and legends, he also dealt in the spiritual arts of palm reading, future forecasting and herbal healing techniques. He taught the children about healthy foods and created interesting concoctions with bananas and peanut butter. Jena was his most enthusiastic helper during these experiments. The whole family was now eating better meals and mealtime was conducted in a more civilized and cooperative manner. Even Charlie had started to show up regularly for mealtimes. Kosen treated Charlie the way a sympathetic older brother would and was able to provide a more stable home life for him as well.

Jena never asked about her parents although she knew that Kosen would receive the occasional letter from the big city of Karta. She did hear Joan and especially Luan asking when their parents would come home. The answer was always the same, "Not yet."

Life with Kosen was more orderly and more peaceful for the whole family until one morning when an unforeseen crisis disrupted the even flow of things again.

Every morning it was Joan's job to take Suni on her bike to the Kindergarten school because it was too far for Suni to walk. Besides, the school for the little ones was on a different street and Joan needed the bike to get to her own class on time. Jena and Hildi, considered old enough, had to walk with Luan and Hildi's older sister to their own school.

When Jena came home that day she found out that there had been a terrible accident. Joan and Suni were hit by a motorbike and were badly hurt. They were both admitted to the hospital. Suni was in critical condition and was not expected to survive the crash.

Jena was in shock and the next few days passed by in a blur. She had to look after herself during those awful days. Luan was constantly in tears and was no help at all to anyone. Kosen was too busy and distraught to look after her.

Then Mammy was there, crying and crying with Johnnie crying as well. It was bedlam. Neighbors came to try to help the family and also offered prayers. It must have helped, Jena thought, because there was good news from the hospital. Joan could come home for her injuries were not as severe. She had something called 'concussion', something that affected the head.

Jena did not understand all of it but was happy that Joan was all right. More good news came soon after that. Suni had an operation and it saved her life. Every one was very happy to hear that, including Jena.

What was not happy news was the fact that Mammy was leaving again. This time she was taking both Johnnie and Suni with her. The worst part for Jena was to hear that Kosen was leaving as well. He had been offered a better job opportunity in the big city of Karta and would be traveling with Mammy.

Jena tried very hard not to burst into tears as she said goodbye to him.

"It is all right Jena", Kosen said gently as he carefully reached out and hugged her. He knew that the only physical contact Jena had ever experienced in her life was when she had to endure corporal punishments from her Mother. Jena could not remember ever being hugged by anyone, not even her mother. After a moment of surprise she clung to Kosen for a long time. Somehow she could only remember her grandmother's hugs vaguely and they seem to be a memory of a distant happy past.

"You will see me again, soon. You are also going to the big city, did you know that?

"I am, I will? Jena cried out.

"Didn't your Mother tell you? Kosin laughed.

"Nobody tells me anything," Jena complained. "Mammy is it true? Are we all moving to Karta?"

"Yes, as soon as we can find a place that has enough room for all of us, the rest of you will come to Karta as well. In the meantime cousin Hiong from your father's side of the family will stay with you. We sold the house to Hiong and his wife and they have agreed to look after you until we send for you." As soon as the goodbyes were over, Jena ran excitedly across the street to tell Hildi all about it.

"Will you be coming back Jena?" Hildi asked tearfully.

"I will Hildi, I promise that one day I will come back to see you."

The anticipation of the move combined with the change in guardianship helped Jena deal with her separation from Kosen.

Cousin Hiong was not Kosen of course but Hiong came with his wife and new baby. It was quite a novelty for Jena and her sisters to have a real live baby in the house. The baby was like a living doll and Jena was happily volunteering to babysit any time.

Since the doll incident when Auntie Liamay had visited, Jena had stopped playing with baby-like dolls altogether. She still played with dolls but they were her own creations. She had made a whole village of tiny cardboard dolls complete with cut-out clothing and matchbox beds. Jena and Hildi would be absorbed in having numerous adventures with their doll village and sometimes they would invite other neighborhood girls to join in the fun. However, now that there was a real baby in the house, that changed the order of things as far as Jena was concerned. She was a fascinated observer during feeding time and during diaper change time.

Time passed quickly for the four Bune children and before the next school year began, they were on their way to be reunited with the rest of the family in Karta, the capital city.

Far away across the ocean, two anxious elders were discussing the repercussions of the accident.

"The doctors had to take her spleen out, Lowe, will Suni be all right?" Apho asked worriedly.

"Oh yes, as healers we both know that the spleen is very important spiritually. We store much of our spiritual knowledge in this little gland. This soul has planned this Old One. You and I did have a discussion about this when she was born remember?"

"I did not understand it then and I do not understand it now. Why does the Goddess allow this child to suffer so much?"

"The Goddess did not do this, you know that. We make our own choices and decide how we wish to live our human lives. Suni has chosen to close one of her spiritual doors so that she can concentrate on her life lessons as a human. If she is able to overcome this handicap in her life she will accelerate her spiritual growth tremendously. This is what she and Jena have agreed to in this part of their contract. At the right moment in their lives, Jena will have gained the higher spiritual knowledge and will offer to help Suni. It will be Suni's challenge then to accept this helping hand or not. It will not be easy for her for she has raised her bar very high with this choice."

"I sometimes wonder my Wise Old friend why we bother to live as humans."

"Well, don't you know? Humans have the most exciting adventures in the whole Universe! With free will, we can choose to suffer as much as we like!"

Both elders began to chuckle as they saw the humorous part of their conversation.

"Besides telling me all about the accident and the impending move, Kosen had written something else about Jena in his letter.

He told me that Jena's imagination was very unusual and that she claims to see a spirit lady who speaks to her. What are your thoughts on that one, my dukun friend?"

"I am happy to hear that she trusts him enough to share that with him. The angel is one of the many spirit guides that the Goddess has sent to guard and guide her. Heaven knows that child sure needed a lot of help in dealing with her family alone. Unfortunately she is growing out of this childhood innocent state when she moves to the big city and will lose this spiritual awareness. Big cities like Karta are usually not a friendly environment for spiritual growth."

"For how long Lowe, how long will she be in this darkness? You and I know that things will get more challenging for her as she grows older."

"She will have the odd sense of awareness but she will not have the knowingness until she awakens to her true mission in life. The next few years will be very challenging indeed for our Lotus child my friend."

"I intend to hasten my next visit. To tell you the truth I am very apprehensive about what I will find there."

Chapter Six

The big city was not at all the way Jena had imagined it. It was dusty, dirty and very, very noisy. Where they were going to live was another shock for the children. Their mother told them that she had found a place for all of them to live together as a family again but she neglected to warn the children that their new home was a rickety, leaky old shed. It was a two-room shed, with a cracked and dusty cement floor and reed matting for walls.

It was Uncle Chan's shed that stood in the yard of his small factory. It was a house actually that Uncle Chan had converted into two parts. The front part of the house was the beauty school that was run by Auntie Tin, his wife. The back part of the house was Uncle Chan's factory where he produced a variety of beauty products such as facial powders and many fragrant lotions. It was a very successful business and it had an old shed in the side yard when he bought the property. He had no idea that his sister would move her whole family into his shed one day. He was very unhappy with her but it was too late by the time he found out and he was unable to evict the whole sorry family, especially when there were six children involved.

It was a very difficult time for everyone. When the four older children arrived, they were told that their Mother was very ill and the family was very concerned that she might not survive. They were ordered to leave her alone and not to bother her at any time. They could hear her moaning in the back room of the shed but were not allowed to see her.

The front room of the shed was furnished with one big bed and a single cot by the only window in the small structure. There was one small desk against the wall with a naked light bulb over it where they were to do their homework. All four girls had to share this room and three girls had to share the one big bed. There was no other choice really and the two smallest ones, Suni and Jena were designated to sleep in the big bed. Luan and Joan would alternate between sleeping on the cot or sharing the big bed with the younger ones.

Johnnie was still young enough that he was allowed to sleep in an infant cot with the parents at night. There was no room for Charlie and he had to share a small room at the back of the factory with cousin Siak who happened to be Kosen's younger brother.

The excitement of living in a strange city soon wore off as the family tried to cope with this new life. Jena had no quiet garden retreat to escape to and she had a difficult time adjusting to the situation. Fortunately her relationship with her siblings had improved because they were all in the same boat of misery and unhappiness. They stopped teasing her but Jena still felt as if no one upon this earth really cared about her. She came to this conclusion after conducting an experiment. She decided to stay out on the front steps of the beauty school one night and wanted to see if anyone in her family cared whether she went to bed or not. She sat on the stoop for hours and watched the traffic go by outside the fence. No one came to look for her, no one came to tell her to go to bed, no one came, no one cared!

Because she was able to move quietly about Jena was able to listen to the adults around her without being detected. In this manner she was able to find out what was really happening and did find out that the uncles, mother's brothers were very upset with their situation. Apparently Kin, her father had been without a job for months and this had disturbed and worried her mother so much that it caused her illness.

The uncles immediately got together and first of all persuaded Uncle Chan not to evict them from the shed. Next, one of them got Kin a job and helped him purchase a tiny car to get to work. They also insisted that the children were sent to school every day. Jena never really found out who was funding that enterprise. It took some planning because the schools were in different parts of the city and it was not possible for any of them to walk to their destinations.

The uncles of course had bigger and better cars. Jena found out that at least two of the uncles, Uncle Chan especially, were considered rich men and had more than one car. Cousin Siak was often asked by the uncles to volunteer to drive the children to their different schools. Cousin Siak was not like Kosen but Jena liked him anyway.

Soon they fell into a routine. They would all be driven to school in the morning and it depended on whose uncle's car was available besides their father's little Fiat. Trying to get home required a long wait, especially for Jena, Suni and Johnnie. The three youngest were enrolled in the Dutch language school to complete their Dutch education and the school was the farthest away from home.

For the next couple of years, Jena learned what the word 'patience' meant. For the first time in her life she hated school and was not able to gain good marks. She could not make friends, she felt like an outsider, someone who did not belong. There was only one tiny amusing incident that first year that relieved one of many dreaded school days.

Jena and her sisters had volunteered to be the practice guinea pigs for the beauty school and a couple of students had permed curls in Jena's hair that year. To her surprise she overheard the whispered admiration of the two ten year old boys behind her when she showed up for class with her new hairdo. They thought her very pretty with her curls and Jena giggled within herself at these silly boys! "Me! They think I am pretty! That shows you just how dumb boys are!" she decided.

In the second year her classmates were mostly beautiful Indos and treated her like an alien being. They had nothing in common as far as the girls in the class were concerned and they did not invite her to join them in all their games or in their girly chattering clutches. She was the youngest in the class and they made fun of her clothes! And yet, Jena loved the Dutch books, she loved the stories of this far away land. She loved reading about something called snow and ice that fell from the sky during a time of year called winter. It was all entertaining fairytales and more fuel for her daydreams. How she wished to be able to see all of these wondrous sights one day!

After the Second World War, the Dutch were ordered by the Allied forces to vacate the country and return the government to the native people. This was completed and in doing so the Dutch people were told to go back home to their own homeland, a country called Holland far away across the ocean. Most of the Dutch schools were closed. Only a few were left open and functioning in the Dutch language to serve the remaining Dutch citizens who were by this time all Indos. There were no more people with white faces, blue eyes and blond hair walking around in the city. The local government gave the Indos, who were considered to be Dutch descendants, a year to leave the country. Jena heard about ships in the harbor that waited to take all the Dutch people away.

Jena knew that she was not Dutch and understood that she was only allowed to be a student at this school because someone paid her tuition. She also knew that she would not be allowed to continue this part of her education much longer. It was only a matter of time and soon it would be against the law to speak the foreign language or even to read a Dutch book.

Jena was sad and wondered why people could not get along with each other and why they had to force people to leave their homes just because they did not speak the same language or did not look the same. She grew up in a hurry and did not feel as if she was home any longer. She did not know what home felt like. Neither her country of birth nor her own family could give her that comfortable feeling of home, of belonging somewhere.

Pho-Pho came to nurse her ill daughter not long after they moved into the shed. It was another sad time for Jena. Grandmother was too busy nursing her daughter and had no time for her granddaughter. Jena barely saw her because by the time she came home from school Pho-Pho was often not at the shed any longer. Uncle Chan insisted that his mother take her time to rest and would drive her home to his house that was at the other end of the city. To everyone's relief, Lian finally began to recover from her illness. She was slow to recuperate because she had lost a lot of weight and was physically and mentally very fragile for a long time. Jena was very disappointed when Pho-Pho left as soon as Mammy was able to walk about again.

During their mother's illness Joan was in charge of feeding her younger siblings. She had to use the small kitchen at the back of the factory after all the workers had gone home. The compound was completely fenced in and there was no place for any of the children to go or do anything. They had to create their own amusements. Jena chose to be in the kitchen because she liked cooking and would try to help Joan as much as she could. Auntie Tin would occasionally come into the kitchen as well, especially when she had to work late. Jena loved Auntie Tin immediately and thought her to be the most beautiful lady in the city. Auntie Tin never yelled or swore. She was a true lady and she was very kind to this unfortunate family, especially the children. As far as Jena was concerned, Auntie Tin was a class act, a truly gracious lady.

Only once did Jena hear Auntie Tin comment on their sorry situation. Jena was in the beauty school, where she was actually not allowed to be during the day, crouched behind some cupboards in search of a specific color of nail polish. Since she had volunteered to be used as a practice subject, Jena was going to persuade one of the students to practice on her nails that day. Suddenly, Mammy and Auntie walked into the room. Jena could not sneak out then and of course she had to try to keep herself hidden.

"Lian I heard that Kin's family is very rich and since Kin is the eldest son, why has Kin not asked for help from his father?" Auntie Tin's voice sounded puzzled.

"You and the children are in dire need of financial help right now. Your brothers and your sister can only do so much because they have their own families to look after."

"Tin, didn't you know that Kin's family hates me? They never approved of our marriage and even accused me of trying to steal their fortune."

"They did not!" replied Auntie in shock.

"Yes they did, and Mother had to face Kin's parents to clear my name. It was one of the reasons that we moved out of the Bune's residence. Kin's father insisted that Kin hand over his wages after brother number two had secured that supervisory job for him soon after we got married. Kin refused and that was another reason for us to move out.

His father was so angry that he disowned his oldest son at that point. They have never seen any of Kin's children and have turned all of their family against me."

"I am so sorry to hear this tale." Auntie Tin said with a sad sigh. After this conversation Auntie Tin never brought the subject up again and patiently tried to help as much as she could.

Back in the midwife's tea-room, Apho continued with her sad report of her recent visit to Karta.

"It hurts my heart Lowe to see Lian and her brood of children living like that. As far as I am concerned they live in a hovel. I really had to give all my other children a good talking to. I was upset that they had allowed their own sister to come to this sorry state of living. One of them finally got a job for Kin and they all chipped in money to send all the children to school. Liamay was just as disgusted as I was with the situation. She is now trying to convince one of her brothers to help her in financing the purchase of a house for Lian and the children. After all we cannot stand by and allow them to live in that shed much longer. The children are growing fast and it is not a healthy situation for all of them.

It was painful for me to see the way it has affected our Lotus Child.

Chan my son would not allow me to stay with Lian of course. There was no room in the shed or I would have ignored him if there was. However I did insist on looking after Lian during the day when the children were in school but Chan would often drive me back to his house before they got home. He was worried that I was overtaxing myself and was worried that I would get sick as well."

"You can't blame him for that Old Healer. I know that the healer within you would keep on working and helping out and not think of your own health."

"I could barely look into Jena's big brown eyes when I did see her. She has become a very serious, silent, and solemn child. There is such deep sad questioning in her eyes. We did not have much time together but I did manage to teach her how to sew and to embroider little flower patterns. She picked it up very quickly and at least it will give her another source of enjoyment. I insisted on spending the weekends with the children while I was there. I know, I know, you are just going to tell me that this is all as it should be, aren't you? It is so hard to understand what the Goddess is up to, Wise One."

Chapter Seven

Many more of Jena's cousins lived in the big city as well. She finally met all of them. Uncle Pin's children who were at the same age level were frequent play companions. Greta the oldest girl was exactly Jena's age. Then there were the three younger boys, two younger girls and later one more baby boy. Uncle Pin built pianos and sold or rented them out to various institutions such as the church and the convent.

Jena had her first encounter with a bad case of jealousy. In Jena's mind Greta had everything she had ever wanted. Greta's mother was an Indo and thus considered beautiful of course. Greta and her sisters followed suit. Although they had brown eyes, they were still blessed with the white skin and brown hair of their mother and thus considered to be the beauties of the family. The cousins had everything, a big comfortable home, all the toys their hearts desired, all the food they could eat and the best schools in the city. Before long Jena and her sisters were faced with the humiliation of having to accept their cousins' discarded clothing. Jena did not mind it as much actually because this way she was at least able to have a decent dress and not a home-made one that was a cast-off from one of her older sisters.

Greta and her brothers thought that is was such an interesting thing for their poor cousins to live in a shed that they came over to play. They had never seen anyone living in a shed before. For them it was a novelty but for the Bune family it was stark reality.

Jena and her siblings were invited to come over once in a while to the big house, but somehow Jena never felt comfortable in her uncle's home. Although they had everything, she realized that no one was truly happy in that household. Auntie Nona was always yelling and screaming at her children and would favor her oldest daughter over the other children. Greta seemed to be getting everything she asked for and was allowed liberties that Jena could only dream of. Greta could go to all the parties she was invited to and could join in many special activities that were available for children of rich families. How Jena wished that one day she could be the one dressed in a pretty dress and be the belle of a party.

The first Christmas in the Big City was a very unusual one for Jena and her family. Jena knew all about the Dutch Christmas of course, the decorated Christmas tree, the special treats and the presents. The school would organize a special day where St. Nicholas, the Dutch Santa and his Black Peter would make his appearance. They would come and pretend to ask the teachers who the good or bad students were that year. Black Peter was Santa's helper and if you were a bad child he would put you in his big bag and carry you off. Where to, Jena never found out but she found Black Peter, with his black face and red lips to be quite frightening. The school children would then get their yearly treats of candy and cinnamon cookies.

According to Dutch tradition, you had to put your shoe outside your door on the night of December the fourth. St. Nicholas would ride his horse from door to door that night and would put a big chocolate letter, usually the first letter of your name, in your shoe if you were good. If you were considered bad, you would find a piece of black coal in your shoe instead. The next day on December the fifth was celebrated as St. Nicholas day and everyone would exchange their Christmas gifts that day.

At nine years of age Jena was aware that Christmas in her neighborhood was a two tiered celebration. One was where the Church celebrated the birth of the Christ child on the twenty fifth and the other one was St. Nicholas Day with all the treats and the presents. Jena's family had never celebrated Christmas because they were not Christians and did not belong to any church congregation. She did not believe in the tale of St. Nicholas coming to bring presents and did not agree that Christmas only belonged to Christians. She decided to take matters into her own hands.

"Why don't we have our own Christmas party? Come on, we all like getting presents don't we and we all know that there is no money to buy any. How about if we make things for each other, please, please? We'll draw names so you only have to make one gift. We can all do it. I will help Johnnie and Suni to make their presents if they need it," Jena promised. To her surprise they all agreed.

Excitedly Jena began to make her preparations. First she asked her aunt if she could have all the old magazines that were lying in the corner of the beauty school. She picked the most colorful pages of the magazine and began cutting them into small triangles. Next she asked Joan for some yarn and began to glue the triangles onto the string creating a garland of tiny colored flags. By this time, her enthusiasm was catching on and the others began to suggest other creative decorations. They hung the garland and any other decorations that were made around the room where the girls slept.

In the meantime Jena was busy secretly embroidering a small lacy handkerchief for Luan whose name she drew. Jena had been practicing her sewing skills on any scrap of material she could find since spending that precious time they had together on Pho-Pho's last visit.

Something was still missing somehow, as Jena surveyed the small room in the shed. The garlands were hung and everyone was busy secretly wrapping their small gifts to each other and yet something was not quite right. Jena didn't know what it was until she saw it!

She was big enough now that she was allowed to walk along the street on her own and Jena took this opportunity to explore the neighborhood whenever she could. On her way home from such an excursion, Jena saw that someone had cut off a big bottom branch from a Christmas tree and thrown it beside the road. It was a beautiful branch and just the right size for the small room. Happy with her find Jena dragged and carried the branch home.

"Look what I found," she cried joyfully. "Now we have our own Christmas tree."

"How are you going to decorate it Jena?" Joan shook her head at this impulsive sister.

"We can make some," Jena suggested and proceeded to show her sisters how to crunch up the pieces of the magazine into tiny balls. Using a needle and a long piece of thread, Jena strung the balls into another miniature garland that was then used to decorate their tree. They were able to find an old pot, filled it full of pebbles and dirt to hold the branch upright and found a perfect spot between the cot and the desk for it. Then Charlie surprised them all be showing up carrying a handful of small candles. Using some paperclips he found, they were able to attach the candles to the small branches of their miniature Christmas tree. It was a marvelous tree and as they found more ways to decorate it, it became more beautiful in their eyes. None of the adults knew what they were doing because no one ever came near the shed. Their parents only came to sleep in the back room and they usually went to bed quite late.

December fifth came and all the children gathered in the shed. Everyone was able to forage little treats from the kitchen. Even Johnnie managed to find some candy. Joan brought a jug filled with juice and Charlie somehow miraculously produced tiny bits of delicious sausages. Jena had some riceballs to go with it and Suni and Luan were able to get some fruit. They all agreed that Charlie, being the man of the party was the one to light the tree.

Jena could not figure out how he was able to procure some matches to do it, but he did, and the tree was lit amidst happy cheers.

Jena watched the faces around her glow with wonder and happiness; it was a very successful party. The homemade gifts were much appreciated. Suni proudly presented Jena with the pencil-bag that she had made with Joan's help and Luan was surprised that Jena could make such a nice handkerchief.

The party would have lasted a lot longer if the candles had been more cooperative. As it was, the children did not anticipate the fact that the candles would burn very quickly and in doing so set the whole tree on fire. Johnnie saw the flames first and started screaming as he pointed to the burning branch. It was an alarming moment as Joan and Charlie tried to put out the fire before the flames would touch the walls.

Joan's quick thinking saved the day when she threw the jug of juice over the tree. It was not the ending that they all expected but they all agreed that it was a wonderful Christmas party despite the fireworks, and they did not mind working together to clean up the mess. It could have been worse. The whole shed was very flammable and they would have lost the only home they had in minutes. Everyone agreed to keep the incident a secret from the adults. Jena shuddered with the thought of the trouble they would be in when her uncle would find out. Furthermore it was her idea and she was the one who brought in the branch. It was a fearful thought! For the next few days Jena kept herself out of everyone's way just in case someone would find out!

"Do you have any news Old One?" Lowe greeted her friend as she saw Apho approaching her gate one fine morning. "Did you have another letter from Karta?"

"Would I come without the latest news?" Apho smilingly shook her head at her friend. "Sin, son number three, has been writing to me. They have finally closed the deal and bought a house for Lian and her brood. The deal almost fell through because Kin refused to agree to pay Sin and Liamay back in installments. It is because third son is such a compassionate person that he persuaded Liamay to close the deal anyway. He told Liamay that he was certain that they would get their money back some time in the future. Liamay was not happy and she told Lian that she was doing it to please me. I am so relieved that the children will leave that shed very soon. I am also happy to hear that Jan, my adopted daughter, will be living with them to help look after the children. Jan is widowed now and needs a place to live. It is a win, win situation for everyone concerned. We both know that Lian is not too keen on housework."

"You and Liamay have actually spoiled her in that area, I think." Lowe reminded her friend gently. Both of you were looking after all the household chores and the children when Lian was living with you. You really did not give her the opportunity to learn how to manage a household. I'll bet that she does not even know how to mop the floor!"

"You are right Lowe and I often regret that fact although I really do not know if I could have done otherwise. I sometimes feel as if she is a child that will never grow up."

"I am so glad that this change is occurring for the Little One my friend. It is definitely time for Ayin to move on to her next lesson. These past two years have been quite heavy and traumatic for her but it was necessary."

"I wish that it could have been done with less pain for her Lowe."

"Pain is not all that bad my friend. Humans remember their lessons better when there is pain and suffering involved. The Goddess tells me that these heavy negative emotions are foreign to the Lightbeings of Spirit where she dwells. It does not exist in the angelic kingdom and it is for them a novelty. That is why they love to hear our stories when we get to the other side. Humans are the only ones in the whole Universe who have the free will to choose to suffer or not to suffer. Pain and suffering are the basic stepping stones leading toward human wisdom."

"I am not sure that I understand what you are saying Old Dukun. I just wish that there was another way to gain wisdom and enlightenment," Apho shook her head in puzzlement as she tried to absorb the teachings.

Chapter Eight

Relief finally came after two years. The children were told that they were moving to their own home. It was not in a fancy neighborhood where the uncles lived, but it was a house with enough bedrooms and their own kitchen. They were told that they had to be very grateful to Auntie Liamay and Uncle Sin who loaned their parents the money to buy the house. The streets were narrow alleyways between the homes but it was not in the poorest part of town and the family moved quickly, with a sigh of relief and gratitude. It did not take them long because there was not much to move. Again the Liu family came to the rescue. The uncles donated beds, furniture and even supplied all the kitchen needs.

Three girls had to share one bedroom again while one of them had to share another bedroom with Auntie Jan who was moving in with them. Jena had never met Auntie Jan. Only recently she had become aware that she was Mammy's adopted sister who was married before Jena was born. Auntie Jan was a poor widow and had nowhere to live. Now she would take over the family's household chores which would free Mother up to do her work. Auntie Tin had graciously allowed Mother to participate in her beauty classes and now Mammy had a certificate as a hairdresser.

A small room at the front of the house was converted into a miniature salon with Auntie Tin's help. With this new enterprise the family's fortunes slowly began to improve. Kin was soon offered another job that allowed him to use his foreign language skills in an exporting company. It was a supervisory position that was more to his liking. Besides, it brought in a lot more money which raised their living conditions a few rungs up.

For Jena the best part of this new house was the small narrow strip of dirt that bordered the house on three sides and to her delight there was a mango tree just outside the side entrance. Jena immediately planned on the many flowers and fruit trees she could plant around the house converting the area into a small garden.

Jena did not see much of her cousins, especially Greta, for the next few years. She did catch a glimpse of them briefly once in awhile while walking on the street, as they were driven by in their car. Jena sadly watched them whiz by and wondered why they never stopped to offer her a ride.

"We are the poor cousins, don't you understand?" Joan told her when she talked about it at home. It is an embarrassment for them to acknowledge our very existence. It is bad enough that we have to visit all of them on every Chinese New Year's day to receive the lucky money envelopes. I hate it every time we have to go." Joan sounded very angry and resentful.

Although there seemed to be enough money for food, the children were constantly reminded that they were still poor and that there was no money for extra treats. Jena did not feel any different and wondered why people would treat others in a condescending manner just because one was poor.

It did not take them long to get settled in the new home. It was slightly better constructed than the shed but some of the walls and the main ceiling were still built with coconut leaf matting. It was sturdy enough and it was porous enough to let in much needed breezes to cool the house down and that was all that mattered. They were lucky to have a house.

Jena immediately chose to sleep in the girl's room and claimed the top bunk of the three-person bunk bed. There was one desk for everyone to share, a couple of chairs and Uncle Sin had also gifted them with a real shelving unit for their clothes. They could now get rid of the produce crates that they had been using up to this point. The whole house had a tile floor that kept the house cool during the heat of the day and doing homework became a lot more comfortable.

Jena had another move to face as well. She had to go to another school. The local government decreed that everything Dutch was now considered foreign and everything was to be closed for good. What everyone suspected came to pass and books in this foreign tongue were ordered burned nor was the language to be spoken in public any longer.

Jena had to enter the local school run by the nuns in the convent. The Catholic nuns were the only ones who ran a school in the city that would provide a decent education for the girls. The nuns were all Catholic missionaries, some from Holland and some from other countries in Europe. Mammy kept telling them how lucky they were that she was able to enroll all of them. The tuition fees were quite high and she was only able to get a discount because of Uncle Pin. Uncle Pin would provide free tuning services for the nun's pianos and sometimes would sell them one at a discount price. There were two convent schools and Jena was enrolled in the closest one, which provided primary and middle school education. Uncle Pin's girls went to the bigger one next to the cathedral. The bigger convent could accommodate the full range of classes, from primary to middle and on to the high school and was considered to be more prestigious. Both Luan and Joan had to go there because they had reached the high school level.

Jena thrived in the new school even though the curriculum and the language were different. All the subjects were taught in the native tongue and although Jena spoke the language she never had formal instructions in it. The nuns called in her mother and suggested a tutoring program for Jena. Lian reluctantly agreed to pay the money for it. From then on, Jena's grades improved and she loved the nuns and the teachers. She felt that the nuns genuinely liked teaching all the students. She felt accepted and loved the tranquility of the convent atmosphere.

She learned a lot more about God this time and was introduced to Mary, the mother of Jesus. There was a wonderful meditation grotto in the middle of the convent just outside of the classrooms. There was a beautiful life-sized statue of Mary in the stone grotto surrounded by blooming flowers. As Jena gazed at the statue, she fell in love with this beautiful lady with the blue mantle. She felt a connection deep within her and knew that this was a special secret she had to keep to herself.

She could hear her mother's warning voice over and over," I want all of you to listen to me, and don't stare at me, Jena, or I'll slap you again. I have no choice but to send you to the convent schools because they are the best girls' schools in town and I want all of you to have a good education. I was lucky enough that my second brother paid for my college education and look what I was able to do for the whole family after I graduated. You have to listen to your Catholic teachers and the nuns' teachings because that is part of the deal of going to school there, but don't get any ideas of joining that religion. I have told you that before! Don't believe in that Christian religion. We are of Chinese heritage from our motherland, China, and we follow the belief system of the Buddha and of the holy man, Confucius. You are not to follow the example of Uncle Pin's family. Your Aunt Nona is after all an Indo and she has the whole family baptized in the Catholic Church because she wants to be part of the so-called rich section of society. We don't belong in that group, so don't get any ideas!"

Jena's relationship with her mother continued to be on rocky ground as Jena grew into her early teens. She soon realized that her parents were both child-like and really did not know what to do as parents. Lian, her mother, really could not cope with the challenges of dealing with four teenage girls and Jena greatly missed having a more loving and supportive mother.

She found the love that she so desperately craved in the presence of Mary, the eternal Holy Mother. This was the beginning of a very close and intense relationship with Mary. Jena prayed and talked to Mary constantly and often felt the closeness of a loving presence. It almost felt as if she could hear the Holy Mother's voice in her head. It sometimes felt as if she had heard this voice before, one that sounded like her own voice and yet Jena knew in her heart that it was Mary, comforting her, consoling and loving her like a Mother would. Jena continued to be puzzled at the strong animosity that existed within her parents against the Catholic Church and knew that she would get into a lot of trouble if they found out how she felt about Mary.

"Come in quickly Apho. You must have some interesting news to share for you to have walked all this way in the rain," Lowe chided her friend gently. *"You will get a cold in this weather soon enough."*

"It wasn't so bad. Besides, I sometimes like to walk in the warm rain as long as it is not a monsoon deluge and the roads have not been turned into a muddy river."

"You are lucky that it has not come to that!"

Soon they were both comfortably sipping the fragrant cups of tea in Lowe's tea-room. "A dash of licorice, lemon and hibiscus blossom in this one?" Apho teasingly looked up at her friend.

"I was hoping to fool you with the strong licorice taste! One point for you again!" Lowe shook her head in resignation. "I can tell from your smiles that all is well with our Little Lotus?" she continued after a few sips from her cup.

"Well, she is not that little anymore, she is twelve years old you know", informed the proud grandmother. "Yes things are a lot better now that they have moved into their own house and now that Jan is looking after the household chores. At least the children are now well looked after and are getting decent meals. Jena is going to the nun's school which is much better for her and I hear that she is doing well in her studies. Lian is worried though that the girls will be brainwashed with all the Christian things they are learning at school. What do you think Lowe?"

"The Goddess tells me that she has to walk this path, Apho. The Holy Mother Mary is now walking with her and will be of much help to her in the next few years. Mary fills in the role of the Mother that Jena sorely lacks and yes she will choose to join this church for part of her life. This church has much to teach her and don't worry she will not forget your teachings."

"I am due for my next visit and I want to find out for myself how things really are in Karta," were Apho's final words on the subject

Part Three

The Sapling Stalk

The Lotus stalk continued its journey growing forever upward
It could now see the light shimmering high above
Its tip moved bravely through the treacherous waters
Every layer it entered had new challenges
The current was more turbulent as it neared the surface of the pond
The danger of being uprooted, of being swept away, was a daily hazard and then it had its first experience of a storm that raged high above the glassy barrier
It could feel the pelting rain drops penetrating its watery world
Drops that transformed into sharp elongated crystal needles
Grazing, hurting its tender skin
Then one day with a burst of energy it breached the surface
With awe the stalk looked around at this new vista
Everything it had ever known was not there any longer
Nothing looked familiar, everywhere it gazed was foreign to its sight
A new world, a new life was unfolding before it
A new growth called a leaf was now in production
A new being was being created.

Chapter One

They were soon settled in the new surroundings and the novelty of it dissipated into the daily routine of school and homework. It was a new beginning for the whole family. They were all in one house now and it was time to learn to get along as a family.

It was to be Grandmother's first visit to the new house and to Jena's delight it was to be a much longer visit this time. Jena tried to spend as much time as possible with her grandmother and insisted that she sleep with Pho-Pho.

"Show me again Pho-Pho," Jena would immediately ask for her grandmother's attention as soon as she came home from school. Pho-Pho was teaching her how to crotchet and knit. Auntie Jan told her what a talented artist Grandmother was and how she taught Auntie Jan how to crochet the beautiful peacock lace bedcover that Jena admired very much.

Time flew when Pho-Pho was there and Jena could barely remember such a happy time as this with her grandmother. She loved hearing the stories of village life on the island and asked wistfully, "When can I go with you back to the island, Pho-Pho? When can I meet Auntie Lowe again? I don't remember her anymore."

Her grandmother could only smile sadly, "Maybe one day when you are older and when you can pay for your own plane ticket, Ayin, you will come back for a visit. You know that your uncles always provide me with the tickets and that is why I can only come once a year to visit you."

"I will come and visit Sungai again, you'll see, one day I will," Jena promised.

It was too short, too soon, as far as Jena was concerned, and she could not understand why Pho-Pho had to go home again. While Pho-Pho was there, Jena had a respite from her mother's temper tantrums for Jena was the only one who was the recipient of all of the corporal punishments Lian would give out. Jena knew of course that her mother would not dare lay a hand on her while Apho was there. Grandmother would not allow it and Mother knew it.

School became a refuge for Jena as time went by. She made some friends and was happily surprised when her friends told her how much they liked her and how much they admired her. Jena could not figure out what it was about her that had her classmates choose her as a leader. She was soon nominated to become the class monitor.

There was only one fly in the ointment and it disturbed Jena greatly when she became the recipient of racial discrimination.

The nuns were not the only teachers at the convent. The other teachers were native-born, graduates of the nuns' teachers' college at the back of the convent compound. Being educated in a Dutch school, Jena rarely had any close encounters with the native citizens of her birth country, except with the village maids. She knew that her forefathers were immigrants from China and had lived in this country for the past five hundred years. Besides the Chinese, there were also immigrants from India and Arabia who were now part of the population.

It was therefore a puzzle for her why there was such animosity towards others not born of native heritage. She understood that there were slight differences in skin color, facial features and cultural customs but could not fathom why it should make any difference in living in peace together.

There were more children of Chinese heritage in the convent than there were of the native-born and this created an uneasy situation in the classroom. It became a very aggressive competition as to which group could get the highest marks. It was another shock for Jena when she found out that her marks were kept at a lower level than her classmates who were native-born. Her friends told her not to complain because it would make matters worse. The teacher was a member of the resistance movement towards freedom from Dutch colonial rule and hated the Dutch with a passion. When she found out that Jena was a transfer from the Dutch school and needed tutoring because she could only read and write in the Dutch language, Miss Tito was not pleased. It was an important lesson for Jena as she had to learn how to face and live with discrimination. Nevertheless, school was still a great place to be and Jena enjoyed learning about everything in sight. She embraced every subject enthusiastically and especially excelled in the mathematics and science part of the curriculum.

Coming home from school not long after her grandmother's departure, Jena was told the sad news that Lowe, grandmother's friend, had passed away. Jena was saddened and wished she could be with her grandmother to console her because she knew how close the two seniors were.

Time went by and as Jena grew older she became more aware of the political situation of her birth country. Things were not peaceful, talks of envy and hatred towards foreigners escalated and it affected the mood of the population everywhere. All the White Dutch settlers were already evicted and now their offspring, the Indos, were ordered to depart as well. More big ships anchored at the harbor to take them away. They had no choice, everyone who had registered as citizens during the Dutch regime were given the choice to leave or to denounce their Dutch citizenship. Jena's parents never registered themselves and the whole family was therefore considered as native-registered.

Against her parents' wishes, Jena began to attend a Catholic church in the neighborhood. She developed a close relationship with an Indo couple who were also members of the church. Jena was very sad when they told her that they had to leave and sail back to Holland, a place that was part of Jena's dreams. Jena had always been fascinated by the stories that she read about these faraway countries where there were four seasons instead of just two, where people wore different clothes, ate different foods and had different activities like skating. She wanted desperately to go with them but was too old for the couple to adopt her and besides she knew that her father would never agree to it anyway. None the less, Jena tried and went with the couple to the Dutch embassy to see if she could be registered. It was a futile exercise! Jena was disappointed and sad. "I don't want to live in this country anymore," she whispered to herself. "I don't belong here! This does not feel like home to me." That feeling strangely had always been there, the feeling of not belonging, not even with her own family. She felt as if she was the foreigner in her birth country.

The sense of unease continued after all the Dutch descendants were gone. The discriminatory focus was suddenly directed to the Chinese descendants. Ugly rumors and frightening messages ran through the Chinese community like wildfire. It did not really register in Jena's consciousness how serious the situation was until she experienced it herself more than once.

She had been visiting her cousin Greta and the two girls decided to walk down the street to visit another friend. They were on the sidewalk when suddenly Jena's intuitive self awakened and hurled a warning signal. Without thinking she stepped off the sidewalk. Two men were walking towards them and when they saw the girls they began to taunt them. Jena trembled with horror as they first started to bombard Greta with ugly, hurtful words just because she was an Indo and had the looks to prove it. At this point Greta noticed that Jena was not on the sidewalk any longer but was trying to walk away from the men. Greta started to turn to follow Jena and that must have infuriated the men because they came after her and started jabbing their burning cigarettes in Greta's arms.

Greta started screaming in pain and in fear as she tried to get away. Without a second's thought, Jena jumped in and grabbed Greta's other arm. She pulled her away as fast as she could and started running, dragging her sobbing cousin with her. Fortunately they were not pursued. Jena could hear the men laughing and was grateful that the incident was happening during daylight hours on a major busy street. For Jena it was sad to realize that the other pedestrians did not even react. No one offered the girls any help, most of them tried to ignore what was happening while some stood still and watched passively. Both girls were shaking with fright and decided not to tell their parents about it. They knew that if they did they would not be allowed to go out on their own any longer.

Jena's intuitive side came to her aid more frequently after that and she learned to pay close attention to the warning signals.

The next attack came in a public bus. There were public buses but they were always extremely full because there were so few of them. Jena was late for school that morning and could not get a rickshaw anywhere. Rickshaws were small carriages that were pulled by a bike-like contraption. She had developed an arrangement with the local rickshaw man to pedal her to school but missed her appointed time because she had overslept that day. She knew how crowded the bus would be but she had no other alternative that morning. As soon as she squeezed into the bus, she knew that she was in trouble. Her intuitive side was screaming for her to get off immediately. The bus however was already moving and she decided to get off at the next stop. She was literally hemmed in while standing in the middle of the bus and was surrounded by native men. There were no Chinese faces in the crowd around her and Jena knew that she had not made a good choice this time. She started yelling at the bus driver to let her out at the next stop and suddenly felt hands clutching at her face and before she knew it someone had grabbed her glasses from her face.

Jena had had to wear glasses for a few years now since her teachers discovered that she could not read the letters on the chalkboard. She was instantly blinded. Her only option was to start making a lot of noise before those groping hands were touching her in other more frightening ways. Guided by intense fear, she started screaming loudly, stomping with her feet and waving her arms angrily, adding more commotion to the noisy rattle of the old bus.

"Someone on this bus stole my glasses and I cannot see anymore!. I need my glasses and I am not getting off this bus until I get them back! I am going to keep screaming!"

Help came from the driver who was getting annoyed with the disturbance in his bus and he began to get angry himself. He pulled the bus over to the side of the road and started yelling at all the passengers. "Whoever it is, give her back her glasses now! I am really fed up with this noise! This is happening too many times on my run and I won't have it any more. I will stop the bus and I am not driving until you give them back. Have you no decency anymore, stealing from a schoolgirl like that?"

"Stop screaming, spoiled Chinese kid, there are your glasses!" One of the men suddenly pointed to the floor of the bus. True enough they had thrown her glasses down and fortunately they were not broken. "You dropped them yourself you dumb Chinese girl!" The man accused her disgustedly.

Jena hurriedly put her glasses back on and scrambled off the bus as fast as she could. Another lesson learned that day and she never went on a bus again.

The next attack came on the street again in a different part of the city. Jena was walking with her friend Ema this time and thought that they were in a very safe area of the city. Ema after all was native-born and was a Muslim. About seventy five percent of the population, including the president, was of the Islamic faith and every mosque in the city would broadcast their call to prayer at the appropriate times every day. Ema had even taught Jena how to sing the first few sentences of the chant. Jena thought it to be very interesting and they were both the best of friends. Ema also went to the convent school because it was the only facility that provided good education for girls. Every family who had some money would send their daughters to the convent. The nuns would accept any girl regardless of their religion or the color of their skin as long as the parents could pay the hefty price the nuns demanded.

By now Jena has begun to recognize her intuitive warnings and she reacted more quickly this time. She noticed a man walking towards them and as he came closer, Jena took one look at his face and immediately turned around grabbing the startled Ema and started running the other way. He was older and faster but Jena had learned to react instinctively. As she felt his hand grasping at her neck Jena kicked back at him and with a burst of speed ran across the street pulling a crying Ema with her.

"Oh Jena, I am so sorry," the trembling Ema sobbed. "Look at you, your neck is bleeding. What are we to tell our parents?"

"We're not telling anyone, promise me you won't tell your parents Ema. I am all right. He took my gold necklace that's all." Jena tried to sound very brave and tried to calm her friend down. Deep inside however, she cried bitterly. It was Pho-Pho's last gift to her, a fine gold necklace that Jena loved and wore constantly.

"This is so strange Jena, I am the one wearing lots of gold jewelry while you have only one thin gold necklace. I don't understand why he would take yours," Ema puzzled as the girls quickly walked home.

That night, Mary appeared in her dream, as she often would every time Jena had a traumatic experience.

"Why, why, is this all happening to me? I loved the necklace. It was Pho-Pho's present, my most valued possession. It is just not fair. Why do they have to be so mean, just because I am Chinese-born?"

"It is only a necklace Jena," the soft voice whispered, "You will have many necklaces in the future. It is not really yours, it belongs to the earth and the Earth Mother. She has allowed you to use it and to look after it for her while you live on this earth. You have to learn that others are not like you and you are now more aware of the darker side of human behavior."

Jena woke up with tears streaming down her face. She did not quite understand the gentle explanation but accepted it because she loved Mother Mary. Her mother had finally given up and ignored the fact that Jena would disappear every Sunday to church.

As Jena grew older, there were more and more happy moments in her life and they were like a handful of brilliant jewels in a basket full of coals. The first few were the ones continuing at school where she was given recognition by her friends and some of the teachers. The church became a peaceful sanctuary for her. Besides attending Mass, she was also the only one of the family who decided to join the Girl Guide organization sponsored by the church. None of her sisters had any inclination to join in any of the activities in which she was interested. They all had a steady routine of going to school and staying home day after day.

Jena could not stand the idea of hiding inside the house and withdrawing herself from life outside the home. The Girl Guide group became a close-knit circle of friends for Jena and it provided her with many happy adventures away from home. During the excursions with her group, she discovered interesting train rides into the mountains and roamed beautiful gardens in small mountain resorts. Jena fell in love instantly with the exotic orchid gardens they went to visit and resolved to buy some plants for her garden.

To her astonishment, Jena discovered that her father was a kindred spirit in this love of plants and flowers. He suggested that they drive up the mountain one weekend and look for some interesting plants. The small car could only contain five people so Jena, Suni and Johnnie were the only ones that came with their parents that day. It was a rare happy moment for Jena as she got to know a rare view of the man who was her father. They brought home a number of plants that day and Jena happily planted them in the small patch in the front yard. It was a very painful awakening, however, when she discovered that the neighborhood vandals had climbed the fence and destroyed her garden during the night. It reinforced her fervent wish to leave this place where people destroyed someone else's property just because they were born different. Jena refused to replant the garden after this incident.

Apho knew that there was a reason why she felt compelled to return home sooner than she had planned. As soon as she had unpacked, she headed out towards the midwife's home.

"Apho, thank the stars that you are here," Lowe's daughter said tearfully. "She has told us that you would be coming today but we thought that you were planning to spend another week with your granddaughter."

"I felt her, Sini," Apho said soothingly. "I know that her time has come and that she is only waiting for me. May I see her now?"

Sini nodded quietly as she mopped her eyes. "I will brew some tea for you in the meantime."

Apho could hear her friend's labored breathing when she entered the room. She sat down in the chair beside the bed and gently touched Lowe's hand.

The old dukun opened her eyes and smiled at her friend, "What took you so long? I knew that you could hear me calling you. I am ready to go, Old One, and I know that you are not that far behind me. How is our Lotus teen?"

"You are not well Lowe, no need to bother you with earthly squabbles, my friend."

"Don't give me that excuse. Since when have we not shared our concerns with each other? This is just a small kink in our lives. I am only going through the door of death to the other side. That does not mean that my mind is gone you know." *Lowe weakly glowered at her friend.*

"I am sorry, I worry about her Lowe. You and I know that the troubles are just getting worse. It has even reached our little community. We used to live peacefully with our neighbors no matter who they were. And now we have to watch our step because of our heritage. It is really bad in the big city."

Lowe's labored breathing turned into a wracking cough.

"There now I have made you worse. Here, drink this slowly," *Apho gently lifted Lowe's head and put a cup of tea to her lips.*

After a few minutes Lowe's breathing became easier and she gazed lovingly at her friend. "Thank you and don't worry about me or about your granddaughter. She is learning all about the dark side right now and is acquiring skills that *will help her greatly. She has made numerous friends and they will be the mirror to show her that she is a nice person and one that deserves some happy moments in her life. I'll be waiting for you on the other side Old One. Thank you for coming to see me off,"* Lowe smiled and with a deep breath closed her eyes for the last time.

Chapter Two

Jena continued to read ferociously and would search through various libraries for books about faraway lands. It was quite by accident that she discovered a small hidden library behind the church, where a number of Dutch books were concealed. She was sent by Father Brian to look for one of the servants when she happened to pass a small room full of books. Jena was very happy with her find. She persuaded the servants to allow her to borrow as many as she could carry and she promised to return them.

It was another happy interlude for Jenna when she found the treasured books. Her favorites were stories about a faraway country called America and the Native Red Indians who lived there. She dreamt about traveling with the buffalo, sleeping in tepees and eating bannock, the Indian soda bread. She could not read enough and would read far into the night by the light of a flashlight at times. Jena did not understand why she felt an incredibly close connection to these special people of the American plains. It was as if she knew them and was resolved that one day she would meet them in person. She dreamt of living among them, in a small cottage in the middle of a sunny clearing in a forest of majestic trees. Old Shatterhand, the woodsman, and Winnetou, the Indian Brave, became her heroes, her models of a life she dreamt of constantly. It became an obsession and a determination that she would see those sights one day.

Jena loved reading her books while she was sitting in front of the only window in the bedroom. Just outside the window she had planted a papaya tree and it gave her a sense of delight to watch the green papayas ripen on the tree.

The bedroom door opened into an inner courtyard that was not so pleasant.

The inner courtyard was where the kitchen sinks were and where sometimes the inadequate sewer system would overflow. Jena found that she had to keep her feet off the floor when she did her homework or read her books because the sewer mice would come out at night and run over her feet if she had them on the floor. Jena shuddered every time she would see a mouse from then on. However mice were not the only nuisance she had to deal with.

Dogs and pigs were considered unclean animals in the Islamic faith and they were shunned by every Muslim neighborhood. A person who came in contact with one or both of those animals had to bathe seven times and spend some time in the Mosque to cleanse him or herself. On the other hand, other neighborhoods with different religions would catch any dog found on the street and it would end up on the dinner table. Cats were the only ones considered suitable as pets and they were allowed to roam the narrow streets at will. Wild cats became abundant and would slink into every home in search of food. Aunt Jan had to be vigilant during the day as she was preparing food for the cats were known to slink in quietly and snatch any food left unattended. They favored fish of course and that was the daily entrée on the menu since it was the cheapest item to be had in the market.

The ceiling of the house was also built with matting just like the bedroom walls and sometimes there were holes that had to be patched quickly. Jena could never forget the night when her dislike of cats escalated. Everyone was sitting down for dinner at the dinner table that evening and suddenly without warning the ceiling above them caved in and carried a screeching cat with it. The cat had been hunting for mice in the attic and unfortunately was crawling along when the ceiling ripped apart. There was bedlam around the table as everyone tried to scramble away from the furiously hissing cat and from overturned dishes of food. It left such a distasteful memory for Jena that she would develop an allergic reaction from that day forward to the presence of any cat.

Geckos, the tiny lizards that lived in every nook and cranny of the house, were a common factor in every tropical home. Jena did not mind them as long as they stayed on the walls and the ceiling. However she had a number of skin crawling occasions where one of them would fall on top of her head. It made the hair on her neck stand up as she screamed for help, for the lizards sticky paws would be glued to her hair and someone had to pry them loose.

Cockroaches were another health hazard. They would swarm into every room at night. Some of them were about an inch and a half long and would invade any area in search for food. The kitchen was the obvious target and Jena was shocked one night when she found her mother there hunting the vermin as she swore at them under her breath. It was not the hunt that appalled Jena as much as the strange delight her mother seemed to have when she caught a cockroach and proceeded to pull it apart piece by piece. Jena felt sick that night and had one of her frequent stomach aches.

"I want to get out of this place, this country and get away as far as I can," Jena promised herself one morning. The cockroach problem was really bad and Jena woke up noticing that they had crawled passed the mosquito netting and had been chewing at the soft flesh under her fingernails. Hand washing became an obsession with all of them, especially Suni, when Jena showed them her bleeding fingers.

It was soon time for Grandmother's next visit and Jena was filled with happy anticipation. She had so much to tell Pho-Pho. She wanted to share with her everything that had happened and that she had not shared with anyone else. "Pho-Pho is very wise and I know that she can help me understand these confusing times," she thought to herself.

With heightened anticipation, Jena was counting the days. It was therefore a terrible shock for Jena when she was gently told that Grandmother had passed away and would not be coming for her planned visit.

Lian, her mother was beside herself, crying and moaning all day.

Apparently Pho-Pho was in the garden picking fruit to make into the sweet treats that were Jena's favorites. She suddenly felt unwell and complained to cousin May that a bug must have bitten her neck. Cousin May suggested that she go to bed and rest and that she would bring her some soup. Grandmother agreed to go to bed, which in itself was unusual. Unfortunately by the time cousin May came back with the soup, Grandmother had already passed on quietly.

The uncles could not leave for the funeral and so they all pulled their resources together and decided to send their sister Lian. "She is mother's favorite anyway," Uncle Chan told his brothers.

It was a painful time for Jena during the time that her mother was away. She turned for solace to the only person she loved right now, the Divine Mother Mary who would listen to her anguished tears and who would never tell her that she was ugly, weird or bad. Her friends did not find her ugly. Instead, they told her how they often envied her because her skin was soft and white.

Jena was baffled why her friends would accept her the way she was but not her mother. She remembered her mother's frequent laments about her ugly daughters and especially one day when Lian was at it again complaining to one of the visiting aunts.

"What am I going to do with the three of them? They are so ugly! How am I going to marry them off?

Thank goodness that Luan has inherited my looks. She is the only pretty one. Mark my words, she will make a good marriage to a rich man soon. I might have to put the others on a tampa and sell them off at the market place." Mother's voice sounded frustrated.

"Lian don't say that," Auntie contradicted. "Your girls are very smart and if you ask me I would much rather be smart than pretty and dumb. Look at the abuse some of the pretty girls have to endure from their rich husbands."

Jena could not help giggling quietly as she visualized the tampa with her two sisters and her sitting in it. A tampa was a big, flat, reed basket filled with produce that the market women balanced on their heads.

When Mother came home from the funeral she told everyone that she was going into the yearlong traditional mourning and that the girls had a choice to join her if they wished. Jena immediately piped up that she would.

"I hope you realize what this means," Mother said. "You must wear only white clothing for the first three months and then for the rest of the year you can only wear white and blue or green. We cannot go to any kind of celebrations or parties either during this year of mourning!" The color white was the color of mourning for the Chinese community and always worn by the family during funerals. Red and gold were for weddings and happy celebrations.

"I understand," Jena replied impatiently. "I love Pho-Pho and I want her to know how much I miss her by doing this."

"You are so silly Jena. She is dead and won't care or know what you wear," her sisters shook their heads at her. "You won't make it for the year, not you, you always like wearing bright colors and like to go out with your friends. You'll never make it!"

"I will, I will, and Pho-Pho is a spirit in heaven now and she can still see and hear me," Jena was adamant. However she did not realize how right her sister's assessments were and that it was not as easily accomplished.

Mother Superior, the school principal, announced that a group of foreign photographers would come and take pictures of the students for a few days. The photos would be sent to Europe where the nuns had their headquarters. It was to show them that the missionary work they were doing was prospering. Mother Superior also said that only those students with bright clothing would be asked to pose for the pictures. She wanted it to be as colorful as can be to show that this tropical school was doing well.

Jena did not mind that she would not be chosen because she was in mourning clothes. What she found so difficult to accept was the fact that Mother Superior quietly chose a number of her favorite students who did not wear bright clothing that day to be part of the group being photographed. It so happened that they were dressed like Jenna in white and blue. Jena did not think that this was right at all and wondered why a nun was allowed to do something that was not fair and break her own rules. Were they not God's special teachers who had to spread his word of truth and love by the example of their lives as nuns? It was a difficult emotion to work through for one who was a newcomer to the Catholic faith.

Mary's voice soothingly whispered in her dreams that night. "Nuns are as human as you are Dear One. They have the same choices and face different pathways every day, like everyone else on Earth. They have chosen to dedicate their lives to the Holy Father and, in doing so, the way they conduct their lives becomes part of the teachings. This episode is being presented to you as a learning situation. It is for you to examine and gain the wisdom from it."

"Welcome Old One, what took you so long?" A gentle spirit welcomed her friend as Apho stepped through the interdimensional doorway that separated the living human world from the earthbound spirit world.

"This is not what I expected at all Lowe. I don't feel any different except that I can't feel my toes anymore. Is this heaven?"

"Oh no my friend," Lowe chuckled. It was not an earthly chuckle but it was the sensation of a chuckle. "You have just passed the tunnel of light and now you have to travel to the cave of creation where you need to pick up the rest of yourself which you left there. It will take you three earth days to go there. After that you have to go through orientation and then I will come and walk you to the last doorway. I am sure that you do not wish to remain in the lower earth realms of spirit."

"Is that why you look so radiant, so full of light? You must have done all of that already. How is it that you are

here in this heavier frequency? Why the three earth days and what do you mean by the rest of me?"

"Questions, questions, every newcomer is full of questions," Lowe's spirit chuckled. "I will answer all your questions as much as I can. Some of them you will find out by yourself soon."

"As soon as I arrived here I asked to be part of your welcoming committee. And yes, you are right, I have passed into the angelic realms where only the higher vibrations exist. Once there, however, we can descend and help any new arrivals. Each must choose to continue to the last gate or to stay here in the lower earth plains."

"Why would anyone want to stay here Lowe? It does not feel right. It is still so dark here. Why are they building homes here just like on earth? It looks like they are trying to live as if they still have physical human bodies. And what are those people doing there standing in that long line-up?"

A gentle smile full of compassion accompanied the soft answer," Many think that they are in Heaven here, Dear One. They can create anything their hearts desire, anything that they could not have when they were alive, and so, they do not believe that there is another doorway. Look over there at that happy young man driving around in his red sports car. When he was a living human he would constantly tell himself, "Heaven is when I can have a red sports car and drive it all day." What they believe in during their life they will manifest it here and think that they truly are in Heaven. The same goes for the homes. How many people have you known in your own life-time who constantly think that a big luxurious house is what would make them happy?"

"The line-up is for people who still believe that they have to wait for the one called Jesus to save them and so they wait and wait and wait. He has come to ask them not to wait any longer but they did not recognize him because he came as himself, the Lord Sananda. The physical form of Jesus is the one they believe in and they refuse to accept the fact that things are different in the Spirit world. These souls are the ones whose minds have been persuaded to believe in a certain way and they refuse to change. Even though angels have come to tell them the truth they still do not believe it."

"You on the other hand my friend, you have already done a lot of spiritual work in your human life-time and have reached a much higher frequency than most people in your village. Besides you are a member of the Goddess Quan Yin's circle and are therefore more aware of the higher spiritual teachings."

"Coming back to the three earth days, let's go back into how we got into our human forms in the first place. You know that we are the children of God the Father and Mother Creator and are therefore Lightbeings of great energy as they are. The human body is a very small container for us. Imagine that you are asked to pour a bucket full of water into one of your smallest wine glasses. It is just not possible. A special sacred place has been created for us who chose to incarnate into humans where we can keep the rest of our spirit essence in safe keeping. That is why everyone who dies travels to the sacred cave of creation to pick up the rest of their spirit being. During that time, you also get to attend your own funeral to see who is there, and, to complete some earthly unfinished business," Lowe chuckled again.

"I am glad that you are part of my welcoming party, my friend. It helps to understand things since I am so disoriented," Apho said gratefully.

"What will happen to our Little Lotus, Lowe?" Apho continued. *"I still feel a very strong connection to her."*

"Yes I know. You and I have been granted the chance of becoming her spiritual guides for the next while. We will walk with her in Spirit and can even hold her in our loving energies when needed."

"I am so happy to hear that and I am happy to be here. To tell you the truth, I was getting very tired of my earth life and I missed you dearly after you left. I know, I know you did come back to visit me and I could sense you and hear you but it is not the same as having a cup of tea together, Lowe."

Both Spirits smiled and radiated happy waves of light as they drifted into the next layer of existence.

Chapter Three

The political situation in the country continued to be unstable. It was no surprise that it began to affect the economic status of the whole nation. This created an increase in the stress levels of many families, especially those of Chinese heritage, as the atmosphere of discrimination was strengthened by resentment and anger towards the more prosperous Chinese community.

It was perhaps the increased stress levels of trying to make ends meet that caused Jena's relationship with her mother to deteriorate even more. With the soothing influence of her grandmother gone, Jena became more rebellious and righteous in her sense of right and wrong. She continued to defy and contradict anything her Mother would say to her.

It finally came to a head. Lian had her own strong set of beliefs and decided that it was time for Jena to learn her role as a subservient female in the male dominated Chinese society. Auntie Jan was visiting her daughters and was not home on that day of darkness for Jena.

"Jena, from now on you must serve Johnnie, your brother, and get him anything he wants without arguing or questioning his request. He is a male and is to be treated as such. You must learn so you know how to obey your husband and serve him accordingly, like a well-bred Chinese wife. All your sisters are already doing it. You are the only stubborn one."

"I will not!" Jena was horrified at the very idea. "Men and women are created equal and are to treat each other with equal respect. He can get his own drinks and meals like everyone else in the family. I will not serve him. It is wrong for you to even suggest such a thing!"

Lian was infuriated at this reply. "How dare you talk to me that way. Stop staring at me, ungrateful child! I am your mother, it is your duty to obey me in anything I say. Haven't I told you that over and over again? You never listen to me, your own mother who is to be respected by her own children! You've been trouble since the day you were born!"

"I will not, and I never will obey when you make such unreasonable demands! You do not know how to be a mother!" Jena shouted, then turned around and walked away, anticipating a slap from her angry mother. It was a big insult and it was much later before Jena realized the impact of her words.

She went to her bedroom and threw herself down on the lower bunk bed, grabbed a book and tried to read to calm down. It did not work, of course. She was too angry and furious at her mother for creating such an unnecessary scene.

Her mother would not and could not allow this to simmer down, not this time. Lian grabbed the swishbroom and stormed into the bedroom. She began to scream almost incoherently as she started to hit Jena's legs with the broom. A swishbroom is made out of a bundle of the flexible thin spines of palm leaves. When swung at the right angle it would sound and work as a whip. Lian was wielding it as such while she continued to screech and demand that Jena get up and follow her orders at once.

After the first painful shock of the whip-like broom connected with her legs, Jena remained utterly silent. She wore a summer dress that only came to her knees and the bare skin of her legs was completely exposed. She ignored her mother's presence, which increased Lian's furor and determination to break this stubborn child forever.

Jena lay on the bed without moving and would not allow any sound of pain or anger to slip through her lips. She held herself very still, clutching her book in her hand. The only sign she gave was the silent dripping of tears that rained steadily on the bed. Jena did not know how long this abuse lasted for she knew that her mother was completely out of control.

Her sisters fled in terror and scattered, hiding in other parts of the house. Even Suni could not help this time as she crouched in fetal position whimpering in a corner somewhere. She knew that her mother would be oblivious to anyone or anything at this point in her rage.

At one point Jena felt as if she was not completely there, the pain of the lashes was a distant angry drone far away. She could almost feel as if gentle arms were cradling her and soft voices whispered," Hang on, it is all right, not much longer, Dearest Child. Be still, this is the last one you'll ever have to go through. No one will lift a finger against you this way again. We are with you. Feel us holding you with our love and compassion."

It seemed an eternity before help came in the form of an unexpected visitor. Cousin Hiong happened to drop in and heard the commotion as soon as she entered the house. She wondered why her aunt was so angry and seemed to be in a screaming rage. She found the other girls in the living room and asked what was happening, but they all pointed miserably towards the bedroom without a word. Hiong rushed into the room and was horrified at what she discovered.

"No Auntie, STOP! Stop at once, can't you see that her legs are already bleeding? Stop it! You are not yourself!" Hiong wrestled the whiskbroom out of Lian's hands and flung it out of the door. Was this red-faced, demented creature her pretty aunt? She could barely recognize her. She did not know that her aunt had such a vile temper towards her own daughter. Hiong had always liked Jena and thought her to be the most interesting of the lot.

Gently Hiong escorted her aunt out of the room and sat her in a comfortable chair in the living room. "Stay here and rest, Auntie, and I'll get the girls to get you some tea." Lian's eyes were glazed and she did not seem to be aware of Hiong's presence at that moment. Hiong quickly organized the girls into getting their mother some tea and told Luan to stay with her. She knew that Luan was her aunt's favorite and was the obvious choice to keep her mother quietly in the chair.

Hiong ran back to the bedroom, "Jena, Oh my ancestors, are you all right? What in the world did you do to push your mother into such a horrible state? This is just horrid I have never seen anyone in such a rage as your mother. Let me help you with your legs."

"It was nothing, Cousin Hiong. Don't worry about me, I can look after myself."

Jena was on her way to the bathroom as soon as the beating stopped. She knew that she had to look after her wounds immediately to prevent an infection and remembered what her grandmother had taught her. First she washed the blood off the cuts with clean water. The pain hit her as soon as the water flowed over the cuts and Jena sobbed quietly. It was not only the physical pain of the cuts but it was also the feeling of utter betrayal, complete rejection and proof that her mother did not love her. "How could a mother behave like that?" she wondered.

She went into the garden looking for the healing aloe plant. She could almost hear Pho-Pho's gentle voice, "The aloe plant is a remarkable healing plant Jena. The juice from its thick leaves will help heal most surface wounds, like cuts or bad burns, and prevent infection from setting in. You can also take it internally every time you have a stomach ache, it will sooth the lining of your stomach. Don't forget to ask the plant for permission first before you take its leaf and then thank it properly.

Plants are living things too and are part of the earth as much as we are."

Jena did just that and felt the sympathetic vibration of the plant when she explained to it why she needed one of its leaves.

No one talked to Jena after the incident and no one inquired about her injuries either. It seemed as if the whole family wanted to erase and forget that traumatic day. No one ever told her father what happened either and he remained blissfully ignorant about the incident. It was fine with Jena and she was grateful actually that the whole family left her alone. Her mother somehow chose not to remember the scenario or was so traumatized herself that she could not remember what she had done. She continued her daily excursions to the market and her daily tea time with the neighbors as if nothing had happened.

Jena could not talk about the painful experience to anyone, not even to Kosen, who had moved back into Karta. He had been married recently and Jena did not want to burden him with her troubles. His wedding was a ray of happy sunshine in Jena's life. It was an arranged marriage, a concept that was against Jena's understanding of love and marriage. "Kosen was lucky," she thought. "He happened to fall in love very quickly with a bride he had never met. "When I am old enough to get married, I will never agree to such an arrangement. I want to get to know the person first and love him before I agree to such a sacred ceremony as marriage." Jena made a pledge to herself then and there that she would only marry with love. She was a frequent visitor to Kosen's home and liked his new wife, Soawie, very much, but this incident was too painful to share with anyone.

Two angelic beings glided quietly to one of the scrying crystals and positioned themselves before it.

"Does this have to happen today Lowe?" Apho's spirit questioned as she directed a painful gaze into the sacred crystal's depth before them.

"I am afraid so my friend. You and I both know that this is important for her to learn. Forgiveness is a very big lesson and once understood, it will propel her into a deeper awakened state."

"Let us just hold her with our energies of Love and Compassion. This way we can shield her from the initial pain and suffering that she has to endure."

"Talk to her Apho, help her as much as we're allowed to when we're this close to the earth's frequencies."

"I will tell her to hold on and that it won't be long for this horrific time to pass. Thank you for melding your Love energies with mine, Old Friend."

"You know that I love her just as much and you heard the Goddess speak the other day, didn't you? We both know now what is in store for this child if the potentials are flowing the way we hope they will in the earth's future."

Chapter Four

Time waits for no one, someone once said, and it marches on despite our human dramas. Grandmother's passing was now only a distant memory. There were more things to worry about as the confrontations between the native Muslims and the Buddhist Chinese immigrants continued to boil. Periodically they exploded into violence. The increased resentments and jealousies manifested even more as the military took whatever they wanted without reprisals from the government.

Every Chinese family in the neighborhood had their horror stories to share and one day the Bune family had to face the same frightening drama.

Jena came home from school one afternoon and found a very quiet home surrounded by a feeling of terror. Jena knew that something was wrong as soon as she got off her rickshaw. She was sneaking into the house through the side door when she realized that there was a man sitting in the living room by himself. That in itself was odd. If he was a guest, then her mother or aunt would be entertaining him with tea and cookies. No visitor was ever ignored in this household. Her mother enjoyed the novelty of being the hostess far too much.

She found Auntie Jan crying in the kitchen and tearfully told Jena immediately to be very quiet. The man was a military officer and had decided that he wanted their house. He demanded that they vacate the house immediately because the house was now his and he was going to sit there until they vacated the premises.

"Your mother has gone to your uncles for help. Your sisters were all told to stay at your cousin's house. You were the only one not home from school yet and that's why I am here to make sure that you are not in danger. We are to stay put and not leave the house because if we do, he'll immediately consider it an empty house and move in. Your father is still at work and he won't be able to handle a situation like this anyway."

It was another strange lesson for Jena. She could not understand how someone could just walk into someone's house and claim it just because they considered themselves superior. The man insisted that they were Chinese intruders and not worthy to have a house at all in his country even though the Chinese community had been model citizens for the past several hundred years.

The hours ticked slowly by as Jena and her aunt huddled in the kitchen by themselves. The two daily maids from the village who came to help with the wash and the ironing were sent home earlier in the day. Jena and her aunt were the only ones holding the fort. Jena peeked around the corner at the man from time to time, wondering what he was up to. It seemed that he had decided to lay siege to the house for as long as it took and just sat there pretending to doze in his chair.

It was very late when help finally appeared. Uncle Chan had been able to pull some strings and showed up with another military man who was obviously of higher rank than the one who sat in the chair. Jena could not hear what was said but the man finally left and everyone was able to come home with a big sigh of relief. Mother told everyone later that Uncle Chan had bribed the senior officer. Considering his rank, the junior officer gave in and was told to release his claim on the house. Uncle Chan also gave him a sufficient amount of coffee money as an incentive, of course. Coffee money was the term to disguise all bribe money that everyone was subjected to everywhere in the city. Without coffee money no one could get any official to complete any document, especially passports and exit permits.

After this episode, Jena found out that her parents had been planning to try to relocate to a better place. It was finally agreed that they would try to send the three youngest children, Johnnie, Suni and Jena, to Singa to live with Auntie Liamay. There was not enough money to make the move as a whole family. Kin did have a well paid job now and was very lucky that he had a very understanding and tolerant boss. It was in everyone's best interest for him to stay in the job for awhile, until there was enough money for the whole family to move. In the meantime, Kin would escort the three children to Singa and try to see if he could find a job there.

Jena was in high school now, in the same class as her cousin, Greta. She did not mind leaving the high school knowing that she would definitely make sure that she continued her education in Singa. She could barely wait to leave. The only regret Jena had was that she could not share her happy news with anyone, not even with her cousin, Greta. She was warned especially not to tell her best friend Ema. Ema was a Muslim, she was told, and might betray them to the authorities. It was a time of fear, of cloak and dagger stuff just like in the adventure books she loved to read, except that it was not fun anymore when you had to live it. They had to leave for the airport as quietly as possible and leave with only one suitcase each.

Everything went as planned and the family was to spread the news that the three children were visiting their aunt in another city. No one was to know the truth that the aunt actually lived in another country. The authorities would without delay send someone to investigate the family's financial situation if they found out and extort more money.

Singa was an exciting city for Jena. The Chinese people were in the majority here and there were Buddhist temples everywhere. She had not seen Auntie Liamay for years and was looking forward to getting re-acquainted. It should have been a very happy reunion with Auntie Liamay instead it turned into another horrible emotional drama.

Jena wondered why Auntie was so surprised when they arrived at her doorstep. She welcomed them nicely enough and told the children how nice it was to see them. At the same time, she was very cool and not very welcoming towards Kin. Jena had her first hint here of the depth of her aunt's hatred towards her father.

It became worse when she was told that the children were all staying with her for an indefinite period of time. To her extreme embarrassment, Jena found out that her parents had not written to Auntie at all. They had not asked her if it was all right for the children to come because of the situation in Karta. And here they were, uninvited, and now unwanted, by a furious and livid Liamay. Jena was stunned. Surely this bitter, sour-faced woman could not be the pretty lady who brought her that wonderful doll so many years ago.

Liamay could not send them home because they only had enough money for a one-way ticket. Kin, their father was the only one with a return ticket which he needed because it was soon obvious that he could not procure a job in this foreign city. He was out of touch with all his so-called old friends, especially when it was known that he had been disinherited by his father.

The first thing Liamay did was to order Kin out of her house. She told him never to come back and to take his son, Johnnie, with him. It was a very painful situation for Jena. Her heart cried out as she watched Johnnie leave.

Jena figured that Auntie must have hated her father long before she was born but at the same time Johnnie should not be punished for it. It was not his fault! He was only twelve years old, how could adults do this to him? She wanted to scream and rant at both of them.

Kin got Johnnie a small rat-infested room in the city. He told Jena that she was responsible for her younger sister and brother. Then he went home. Jena wanted to howl in anger but instead had to hide the tears as they rushed like a mighty flood inside of her. The burden was heavy on her shoulders, so heavy that it fell to Suni to take the bus every day to bring Johnnie food and to make sure that he was all right. Jena would break down in tears every time she thought of where Johnnie had to live. "I am only sixteen. I cannot do anything to remedy the situation! My hands are tied by tradition and the lack of funds," she silently lamented. Auntie insisted that they pay for their living and their high school expenses. Mother had provided a minimal amount of money and goods to begin with but Jena knew that it was far from sufficient.

Johnnie had to take the bus to the same school and they could at least meet every morning and stay together during break time. Their father had enrolled them in a school for misfits as far as Jena was concerned and she had another nasty revelation on her first day. Her father had registered her at a very low level because he told her that he did not think she knew enough of the English language that was spoken in this country. He would not and could not accept that she had studied the language in school and could read at high school levels.

Jena begged the principal to allow her into the higher classes when she was escorted to a class that was, not one, but three years behind the one she was in at the convent school. The principal told her that if she could show him at the end of the year that she could handle the curriculum and obtain top marks, that he would consider her request. It never materialized, for the Principal, who was an Anglican priest, was getting paid big fees as long as they were enrolled in his school, because they were foreign students.

Jena was in a class of students who were at least three years behind academically. Her classmates were naturally in awe of her and called her 'Princess'. Her teachers did not know what to do with her and finally decided to give her the 100% marks that no other student had ever achieved in this school. Even with this evidence, Jena was still denied her request to be allowed to join the higher classes. The only reason she showed up in class every day was to get away from her aunt, and out of necessity, because she would lose her student permit if she missed too many classes. In the end, her English teacher assigned her the job of tutoring the other students and marking their papers.

Jena felt as if she was in suspended animation as far as her studies were concerned. "God must want me to learn something different," she thought, "Because academically, I am really not learning much!"

"Poor Liamay, she is still so very angry at Kin. I am glad that you never told me what happened between them, Lowe. My human form would have been devastated had I known of his intentions. I did suggest that Lian divorce him at one point."

"You must have been at wits' end to do such a thing, Old One. Divorce is frowned upon and not recommended in our community on earth."

"I had run out of solutions at that time. I felt that the children would have a better life without his influence."

"It is now Liamay's turn and she has been given the opportunity to forgive her brother-in-law. She has free will and it is too bad that she is not taking this chance in this lifetime. Instead she is increasing her karmic debts by refusing to help Johnnie as well. He reminds her too much of Kin, the father, and in her state of wanting revenge, she has transferred her bitterness to the innocent son."

"I understand and of course she resents not having her own sons with her. She misses them dreadfully. Instead of being there to help her they have both abandoned her. Her oldest was recruited by the Chinese government and moved to mainland China without telling her. He is held there and will never get out. Liamay tried everything and paid a large sum of money to get him released, but to no avail. He is an engineer and the Chinese government will not release such a valuable citizen."

"Left with one son to love, she spoiled him shamelessly and he insisted that she pay his way to study in England. She keeps sending him money and treats every month. He should have graduated by now and should be home helping his mother but I see that he has lied to her. He has neglected his schooling and is having a great time traveling with his Italian girlfriend. Cousin Han actually suggested that she demand an accounting of his expenses but instead she kept sending all the extra money he has requested."

"She is afraid, scared of losing this son too. By giving him all the money she has, she hopes to bind him to her. In the meantime, she is depriving herself of using the money for her own physical comforts."

"There is nothing we can do for Liamay. She has chosen her path and she will soon join us in this world. Right now our job is to keep an eye on Ayin. Have you noticed that Ayin's anger at her parents is thickening the veil around her? It will be harder for her to hear us."

"Don't worry Lowe, she might not hear us any longer but we can still guide her, through other channels. And besides, there is a higher entity here who will strengthen her connection with Ayin."

Chapter Five

The original intent to move to a new and better life had not been realized for the three children. Life in Singa was not much different than their existence had been in Karta. They were still in the tropics, the food was the same and the people were still the same, except this time the Chinese held the majority. The difference was that there was no racial discrimination and it was a safer city. And, there were more Buddhist temples than Mosques in the city.

Life with Auntie Liamay was not much different either, except that Jena was never slapped, or beaten with a broom again. This household was just as sadly dysfunctional as her home in Karta. There was not much happiness and love present in this dreary place. There was no garden retreat. The front yard was covered with a wooden framework that would support numerous trays filled with drying mungbean flour and there was no room for a flower garden at all.

As soon as Auntie Liamay realized that she had no choice and that she was stuck with two teenage girls with no money, she decided to take advantage of the situation. After all, she did need more hands to help with the cottage industry that she ran from her home. The servant, named Saria, whom she had hired many years ago, was the only helper and she was not getting any younger. Saria lived in the house as well and was part servant and part family member. She was a blessing for the girls for she would quietly try to make their lives more bearable.

First there was the bakery and both girls were assigned a schedule. They would alternate getting up at five in the morning to turn on the ovens and start the daily baking. Liamay had arranged a means for the girls to earn some money to pay for their living expenses. Room and board were not free they were told and they had to work for it. They had to bake coconut cakes that cousin Han was nice enough to deliver to the stores in the city every morning.

School began at eight in the morning and the girls had to be ready to walk to school by seven thirty. As soon as they came home at four their chores began. Jena and Suni quietly made up their own schedule and tried to support each other. On top of helping in the bakery, they were also expected to assist in the small factory that produced mungbean flour. Their job was to pound the white flour into small paper tube-like bags until the bags looked like four inch long hard bullets. In order to achieve this, they had to use a hammer and a wooden dowel with the same circumference as the tube. The first attempts were trying times for both girls as Auntie

Liamay swore and yelled at them every time they did not get it the way she wanted it done. Then the flour tubes had to be glued, sealed and packed in boxes ready for shipping to different stores in different cities.

Liamay assumed that Lian had taught the girls her sewing skills and ordered Jena to start on the sewing orders that were part of her means of income. Jena tried desperately to explain to Auntie that she would love to help her but that her mother had never taught her how to sew. What she knew, Pho-Pho had taught her on her rare visits and she also had picked up a few skills from her older cousins. Auntie did not believe her and told her to get started. The pattern was already cut and Jena had to sew all the pieces together. It was an order for a kebaya, the traditional native blouse that all native women wore and that it was also the dress choice of older Chinese women. Auntie was wearing it all the time and so was Pho-Pho. It was a complicated pattern and Jena had never attempted one. It was a disaster! Jena could not get the pieces to line up properly. Auntie swore and yelled and flung the offending kebaya at Jena's bowed head but did not ask her to sew again after that.

Jena soon found a beautiful small Catholic church on top of a hill not far from home and began to attend Mass every Sunday. Auntie was not happy at first but as long as Jena did it quietly and it did not interfere with her chores, Liamay ignored her disappearing acts on Sundays.

Jena always offered to go with her aunt when she wanted to visit a Buddhist temple, but somehow Jena did not enjoy it and was glad that Auntie did not go that often. Jena found the temples very noisy, with sounds of cymbals, gongs, tambourines and the constant chanting. She could not understand the chants but that was not the worst part. The drifting, swirling smoke of the hundreds of burning joss sticks before each statue was overwhelming. One huge statue of the Buddha was the centre piece and a number of smaller statues of other deities were also present. Jena had no idea who they were and she did not bother to ask because the cloying scents of the joss sticks were making her nauseous. She usually had a headache by the time they got home.

In contrast the Catholic Church was very quiet. It was one that was dedicated to the Holy Mother and it was the only place where Jena could find solace and peace. She would light a candle and kneel for hours before Mary's statue. Jena would gaze up at her adoringly. How pretty she was, how beautiful her blue mantle and how lovingly she seemed to gaze back at Jena. Here she bared her soul and cried out her pain and felt the Mother's gentle caress and compassion.

Secretly Jena enrolled herself in a catechism class in preparation for baptism into the Catholic Church. She knew that she would get into big trouble if her family found out, but felt the calling so strongly that she was prepared to face whatever punishment she had to endure. Suni was the only one who knew, because Jena needed Suni to cover for her in order to go to the evening classes. She wanted desperately to belong to Mary's family and the only way to do so was to become a member of her Church.

Jena carefully saved enough money to buy herself the required white dress and snuck out of the house on that special Sunday morning. Jena had told Father Jack that she did not have the required godmother to stand beside her for the ceremony. So Father Jack had asked a member of the Church to take this role. The lady agreed and came to meet Jena just before the ceremony.

The nice lady introduced herself to Jena and then dropped a bombshell at Jena's feet. "Hello you must be Jena. Father Jack told me about you. I am happy to stand as your godmother this morning. It is wonderful that you have chosen to be baptized. I am surprised that your Aunt Liamay has given her permission for it. She is a good lady, your Aunt, and please give her my regards."

Jena never saw the lady again after that day and could barely remember the ceremony afterwards. She kept her mind from the horror that would be waiting for her when her aunt found out by wondering why so few chose to be baptized that morning. She also recalled what the nuns had told her. They said that only those who are Catholics will go to Heaven, all others will go to Hell, the most dreadful place, where the devil lives.

Over and over the following questions tumbled in Jena's mind. "Why are there not more people lining up if that is the case? Why are people choosing to go to Hell instead, and that includes my own family? Am I doing the right thing? There must be a different kind of heaven for other people. There are many good non-catholic people here and I am sure that God would not send them to Hell for the religious choices that they make."

The deed was done and there was no return, no going back. It was not long before the storm broke over Jena's head. Auntie liked to do the delivery of the baked goods herself for it was an opportunity for her to meet the rich ladies who often ordered the sweet treats from her. It was obvious a few days later when she came home from a delivery that Liamay had encountered Jena's most recent spiritual godmother. She called for Jena as soon as she entered the front hallway and the storm broke loose.

"You insolent, ungrateful girl, how could you do something like that behind my back! After everything I have done for you! Is this the thanks I get for taking you in? You made me look foolish and lose face before these ladies because I did not know anything about it. How dare you join that Church knowing that it is against your family's belief system? We believe in praying to our ancestors and to the Buddha. We do not believe in the Christian teachings, they are all lies! I am tempted to throw you out of my house this very minute. The only thing that is preventing me is the fact that the community will think that I am at fault and think badly of me!"

Then came the final blow.

"And here I thought that I wanted to adopt you as my daughter. You are a stubborn, stupid girl and I am glad that your father would not allow the adoption. You are turning out to be just like your silly mother, spoiled and willful. What was I thinking of?"

The apology did not help and neither did the bitter tears. Yet, in spite of the verbal abuse she had to endure, Jena did not regret her actions. Auntie gave her the cold shoulder for days until cousin Han calmed her down. Somehow cousin Han could always bring Auntie out of her angry mood swings.

Every scene flowing through the seeing crystal was observed with interest by the two spirit guides.

"She sure has a stubborn streak in her, this granddaughter of yours," Lowe chuckled.

"I know that she needs to work with this church for awhile. I only wish that she had chosen an easier way to do it instead of aggravating Liamay and causing such an angry reaction."

"She won't belong to it for very long, as you can see, she is already questioning some of their teachings. She has to understand that each religion assumes that its members are the only ones going to heaven. The Muslims have their Heaven and the Buddhists have their Nirvana and the Protestants think that their Christian Heaven is better than the Catholics' and so on. This will help her gain the wisdom in her later life as she will be presented with many spiritual theories and beliefs."

"I see that some of her spiritual lessons are presented during her time at school. What do you see here Lowe?"

"Watch her react to her peers, Old One. She is also learning what it takes to be a good teacher for she will be one herself. Criticisms and judgments are also part of her lessons during this time. She is learning to accept her fellow classmates as her equals and not as the inferior students that the teachers are telling her."

Chapter Six

Jena would always suspect that her Aunt somehow had a hand in the next scheme because of the baptismal incident.

Out of the blue, Jena was told that a marriage had been arranged for her. Cousin Fune was the one who had made all the contacts and the negotiations. Fune was married to a very rich man and lived with her children in a large villa on top of a hill. She told Jena that they wanted to create a closer alliance with one of their business partners by marrying her off to one of the sons.

"I am only eighteen," Jena protested. "I do not want to marry anyone, especially someone I do not know and who is at least twelve years older than I am!"

"Don't be difficult, Jena! For once, obey your elders! Your parents have already given their consent. The young man has agreed and as soon as he can, he will be flying home from Holland where he is in charge of one of their stores." Auntie sounded exasperated. "Don't you want to help your family? Once you are married you will be very rich and you can help your sisters and brothers leave Karta and move to a better country. You have no prospects right now. You will graduate in a few years and then what will you do? You have no marketable skills. You are lucky that they would even consider you, since you are no beauty."

Jena was angry, furious and devastated. "I will not be manipulated and forced into an arranged marriage! I will never agree to this!"

"I told you how difficult she can be," Auntie complained to Fune

"She'll come around, you'll see. Especially when she sees what money can buy, I am sure she'll sing another tune," Fune answered. "You have no choice Jena, your family is counting on you!" Cousin Fune addressed her rebellious cousin. "You are a part of my family and you will anchor our part in this business deal. There is a lot of money involved you know."

"What are you going to do Jen?" Suni whispered anxiously. "You are not going to leave us here after you get married, are you?"

"Don't worry Suni, I will not get married. I promise you and Johnnie that I will keep looking after you."

Jena could never understand how cousin Fune could be so heartless towards them. She knew how poor they were and yet never offered to help, not even to help Auntie Liamay. Fune rarely came to visit but sometimes did order sweets from the bakery. She did so for her daughter's birthday party and invited the girls to come over. Jena assumed that they were being invited to join the party. She was sadly mistaken. They were not even allowed to enter through the front door. Auntie kept reminding them to pay attention to their manners and behave accordingly which meant to be completely subservient to the cousins. They had to enter through the kitchen doors and the girls were allowed a quick peak at the beautiful room where the party was being held and then they had to go home.

Jena was often disturbed at what she noticed around her and would lie in her bed at night wondering why the world had to be so uncaring. "How could people not have any compassion towards others who are in need? How could you ignore your poor family, especially an aunt, your own flesh and blood who was in so much need? Where is goodwill towards all men? Aren't we all children of the same God? What does it matter what color someone's skin is since everyone has the same red blood and the same number of limbs? And what does ugly mean? If God created such beautiful flowers and birds how could he create ugly people whom he considers his children?

She remembered how Pho-Pho used to tell them stories and sometimes she would slip a lesson or two in. "Don't forget that the queen is just a person like us and that she still has to go poo and fart," Grandmother would say with a twinkle in her eye. "Ooh Pho-Pho phewy," the children would giggle and laugh. "You are using naughty words." A ghost of a smile touched Jena's lips as she recalled those happy times of laughter.

Jena realized that worrying about the lack of compassion in the world did not help her present awkward situation. Day after day she would intensify her prayers to Mary, begging the Divine Mother to intercede. "I know that you can do it Holy Mary," she would pray. "Please ask God the Father to help me. I do not want to marry this person even though I am told he is a Catholic as well. I know that God will listen to you. He is God the Creator and can do anything in this world he created."

Jena felt as if there was a noose hanging over her head as the adults refused to listen to her pleas. The family even sent Uncle Pin to try to talk some sense into her. Both parties had agreed and the documents were to be drawn up by both lawyers. There seemed to be no way out.

In the meantime, in the midst of all this commotion, Auntie casually mentioned that she had to have some surgery done in the next couple of days. Nobody suspected that Auntie was sick. Jena thought that she was just being her unhappy, grumbling self. Auntie rarely smiled and the girls had yet to hear her laugh out loud.

The doctor wanted a family member to accompany her and Jena took time off school to look after her Aunt on the appointed day. Jena sat in the waiting room of the hospital for hours wondering what was wrong with her aunt. When the doctor finally came to find her she knew that he did not have good news to share. "Your Aunt is very ill. She has advanced cancer and there is nothing we can do for her. You had better call her son home."

With that prognosis, things changed again. Jena was sad and felt very sorry for her Aunt. "She must have known, Suni," She told her sister. "She does not want anyone else to know and told me to keep it a secret. She did say that she will write to her son and ask him to come home." Jena found out much later that Auntie did write the letter but did not tell her son how short her time was and so he took his time coming home.

There was no more talk about the arranged marriage although Jena knew that Fune did not stop the negotiations. There were other worries and the girls had to shoulder a heavier load since Auntie could not do many of the chores any longer.

The secret could not be kept from the family for long and Fune found out almost immediately when she came to visit to discuss the details of the marriage contract. She took Jena aside and told her that they should move the wedding date forward so that Auntie could have a chance to be there.

"I told you I am not marrying this man. I don't care about your plans. You just want to get more money with this alliance and I will not be part of it! " Jena cried in despair.

"Yes you will! We still uphold our Chinese customs here and your parents have full rights over you. They can order you to get married, which they have by the way, for I have the papers to prove it."

"What else could go wrong now?" Jena cried out hopelessly. Perhaps it was for the best that she could not foresee the future for another storm loomed on the horizon of Jena's life.

"I am glad that it is Liamay's time to come home," Apho whispered compassionately. *She is so unhappy in this lifetime*

and wraps herself in a suffocating sense of suffering. She will not choose to cross the crystal doorway will she Lowe?"

"You can see for yourself Apho, she will need a lot of healing. She is very stubborn and has a very strong ego that has prevented her from seeing the importance of forgiveness and love. On the other hand it is interesting to watch Ayin handle the arranged marriage idea."

"I am surprised that Lian has agreed to this proposal. She was always defiant in the face of my attempts to arrange a marriage for her and insisted that she would choose her own husband. Ayin is too young to deal with such a relationship issue. Besides, what happened to her frequent harping on the fact that the older girls be married off first, especially Luan?"

"My dear look at Lian's thought patterns. Money is involved here and she can see how Jena's marriage will benefit her living conditions. You know how money matters a great deal to Lian. She rates everything around her according to how rich a person is."

"Don't worry. For look, the Holy Mother has already planned a rescue mission. An ingenious one if I might say so myself," Lowe chuckled knowingly.

Chapter Seven

For the next few weeks Jena and Suni were busy trying to cope with the challenges of extra chores and worrying about Aunt Liamay's illness. It fell to Saria to attend to the patient and do the nursing part. The girls had to keep the bakery running and on top of all that both had to keep up with their school work. There was no time to listen to the news on the radio or even to read any of the local papers. Jena was vaguely aware that there were some problems between the two neighboring countries and that the diplomats were busy dealing with it. It was therefore with a sense of foreboding that Jena went to the immigration office after receiving an urgent summons to appear at once.

"Did you not listen to the news?" The immigration officer was irritated and impatient when Jena told him that she had no idea why she was summoned. "My country has declared war against your country and as of this morning the border has been closed. Your inferior country thinks that it can win this war against a stronger and superior force. The English Navy has been deployed under General Lord Mountbatten and is already putting up a blockade with his great warships. All the trade routes are now under our control.

"As of this moment you and your brother and sister are considered enemies of the State. You are ordered to leave this country immediately or we have to incarcerate you and put you in a prison camp until this war is over. The only avenue for you is to fly to a neutral country to the north and then from there find your way south to reach your homeland."

Jena stared at him incomprehensibly as his words flooded her mind. "I, I don't have money to pay for such a journey," Jena stammered.

"Your finances are not our concern and because you and your siblings are teenagers we are giving you one week to leave before we come looking for you."

Aunt Liamay was speechless with anger and worry when Jena brought home the devastating news.

"How in the world are we going to manage that in one week?" she cried angrily.

Jena had no answer for her.

That night as Jena fell into a troubled sleep, the Holy Mother appeared before her in a dream. "There is nothing for you to worry about Dear Child. I will be with you. Don't be afraid you have many helpers and you will arrive safely home," the soft beautiful voice was a balm to Jena's frazzled nerves. Mary's visit brought the peace of mind Jena needed to sustain her in the next trying days.

Help came quickly through one of Auntie's acquaintances. Mr. Jung worked in the harbor and had many contacts who were aware of the situation. He was able to persuade one of the regular smugglers to smuggle some passengers through the border. Auntie was tight-lipped when she paid the fee for three people. Jena could not help that she had no extra money to give. Whatever she had saved would be needed for the trip. They had no idea what to expect and had to prepare for any expense. The smuggler told them that he would take them to the first island across the border and then they were on their own.

"You can only take one suitcase each," Mr. Jung told them. "You must be able to carry it yourself. There is no one to help you. Once you get to the island, you have to find your way to the next island and head as far south as you can. Follow the smuggler's directions carefully. He knows what he is doing. He has done it many times before. Smuggling people across the border is part of his livelihood."

It was a misty, dreary day as the rising sun tried to penetrate the fog that morning. The three teenagers and Auntie Liamay gathered unhappily at a shadowy hidden corner of the harbor.

"Go quickly. He is waiting for you," Auntie said without smiling when Jena tried to say something to her. Jena wanted so much to hug her aunt and to thank her and say goodbye but Auntie would have none of that.

They descended to the lower dock where the smuggler was waiting for them in his sampan. To their surprise, they encountered four other people already hidden in the sampan. The sampan is a long Chinese fishing boat with pointed bows at both ends. It had a reed-covered small dome-like structure in the middle of it and they were all asked to hide under this small canopy.

There was an elderly couple, a man and his wife who were also told to leave and two men in their early twenties. The old man was ill and could not walk. It became the responsibility of the three young men to carry him throughout their hazardous journey.

They sat huddled on top of their suitcases with the old man lying in the centre, and were told to be still. The smuggler told them that they had to pass all the English warships in the harbor before they could reach the open sea. He said not to worry because he had made it a point to travel this stretch pretending to be a local fisherman on his daily fishing run and that the sailors knew him by now.

They were soon on their way and the sampan chugged slowly away from the pier. The smuggler began carefully to maneuver his boat between the warships. Jena was curious and started to peek out but was immediately reprimanded and told to stay out of sight. It was however enough of a peek to fill her with fear. They were very close to the huge towering ships. All she had been able to glimpse were great expanses of black painted surfaces which were the sides of the ships. The smuggler seemed to be known to the sailors who were leaning over the ship's railings high above them, for they hailed the little ship with friendly banter.

"Hey, Hussein, out fishing again? You barely caught anything yesterday. It's too miserable a day to go out.

Don't you ever take a break?" The sailors chuckled as they peered down at the lonely fisherman.

"Yes, yes. I have to make a living you know. I have a nagging wife and if I don't go out every day I will find a very unhappy wife at home," Hussein quickly answered.

"Go on and pass to the left or you'll hit one of our traps in the water then your wife will really get mad at you!" The sailors laughed loudly.

Hussein smiled at their laughter and waved his arm at them as he carefully followed their directions.

Everyone under the canopy heaved a big sigh of relief as they headed to the open sea. It was not a very long trip to the border and they slipped through quietly after a couple of hours. They reached a small island and Hussein headed to a stretch of empty beach and told the four young passengers that they had to get off the sampan there.

"Take that path between those trees and keep walking until you get to the village on the other side. I cannot take you there in full daylight. I will take the two old people to the village inn. I have a story ready to prevent suspicion. Turn to your left towards the ocean when you get to the village and don't talk to anyone. My friend has a small inn there and he is expecting you. The village people will ignore you because I have given them all some coffee money." Hussein instructed them.

"There are no border patrols right now because it is a very small island. They only come once every two weeks to check. Strange, even with this so-called war going on, these men don't bother coming to check the area so close to the border. I guess they are not getting enough coffee money and don't want to be bothered doing their job," Hussein informed them.

It was now a sunny afternoon. The four of them jumped into the warm blue ocean and waded to an expanse of pristine white sand. Jena noted how beautiful the area was. It was as if she had stepped into a picture perfect scene of white sand as far as the eye could see, framed by swaying coconut trees under a shimmering blue sky. How she wished that they were there under different circumstances so that they could enjoy such a beautiful place.

It was at this point that Jena came to the realization that she had just been saved from a dreadful arranged marriage. "What a strange solution this is. How wonderfully the Holy Mother looks after me. A war, just to get me out!" It was a humorous thought and she sent a grateful prayer of thanks into the heavens right there and then.

They were in luck. The innkeeper told them that the weekly ferry that would take them to the next island was due in the next day.

The sampan group of seven boarded the crowded small ferry with some locals and their livestock, in the form of chickens and ducks, the next morning. In no time, they were motoring across the blue ocean waters. Finally, they had some time to get to know their traveling companions. They all had the same story to tell each other. All of them were deported from Singa because of the war and, just like the Bune children, did not have the funds to pay the high prices of a plane ride.

Hanli was a young man about twenty-five years old and was in Singa trying to establish a business deal. He was the oldest among the five younger ones and decided that it was his duty to take charge since he was the senior male member of the group. The elder couple was not taken into account since they were relying on the young to help them throughout this voyage.

This was Jena's first time in the company of a young man and at first she began to fantasize and wonder if there could be a romantic interlude for her here. She was therefore astonished at her own emotional reaction when she did not feel that romantic shiver she experienced while listening or reading her favorite romantic novels. She tried very much to get along with Hanli, although she began to find him increasingly overbearing as the days wore on. However, she realized that they needed him. No male would deal with a female in a Muslim country and Hanli would have to represent them in their journey.

Soto was twenty and was visiting relatives when he was caught in the war. Soto was very compliant and would agree to anything the group decided. Jena thought that he was quite a weak link in the group and treated him the same way she would treat Johnnie, her brother.

It was a good three hour ride to reach the much bigger island and this was where they ran into big trouble.

Another Spirit of light glided gently to join the two regulars at the crystal portal and smiled at them lovingly.

"Welcome Mother Mary," both were pleased at her presence and made room for her to join them at their vigil.

"She is about to face another trial, isn't she?" Apho asked.

Mary nodded, "Yes, look at that frame over there. I will be with her in a stronger fashion this time around. We are so very proud of her. She has met all of our requirements bravely and courageously. The Lady Quan Yin and I are very pleased that Ayin has called me in to help her. As you well know, we cannot interfere unless the one in human form calls us directly for help."

"Both of you may assist me this time with your loving energy. I am to be the main focus here, for the heavy dark male energies that Ayin is about to encounter, will require an intense overlight of Divine Love."

Both elders bowed their heads in complete agreement. "We are so honored and happy, Holy Mother, that you have come in Ayin's aid. We see the darkness that is already moving in for a challenge."

"Quan Yin and I represent the Divine Feminine energy and we will cocoon her within that Light of the Mother God. She will be safe for no darkness can touch her in this protective shell of Love."

Chapter Eight

The border patrols were stationed on this island as well as the customs department and the immigration department. Someone must have passed on the word of their arrival for they were arrested as they came ashore. There was no way they could hide, for it was visually obvious that they were not part of the local population.

"Where are your entrance visas?" demanded the customs official as he scowled at them. "You have entered the border illegally."

"We don't have any," Hanli replied. "We were deported from Singa because of the war. The embassy was closed and so was the border. We had no money and no choice but to hire a boat and come home. We are not foreigners. We are citizens of this country, just like everyone here."

The official would not accept Hanli's explanation, "We are placing you under house arrest until further investigation. We do not believe you and because of the war we are suspicious as to your motives of taking such drastic measures. We are transferring you to the local police department who will decide what to do with you."

They were escorted to a small inn not far from police headquarters and were not allowed to leave except to shop for food supplies. A guard was stationed before the inn's gate and would check their movements during the day.

No one in the group expected this to happen and they were fearfully discussing what to do next. Jena volunteered to look after all the meals with Suni's help and they all agreed to chip in money for their daily expenses. There was an open inner courtyard in the centre of the inn, and all the rooms, including the outdoor kitchenette, were facing this small central garden.

Mr. and Mrs. Woo, the elderly couple, were settled in one room. They rarely left their sanctuary during the entire time that they were at the inn. Mrs. Woo would only come out to collect their food during mealtimes or do some laundry and sometimes help with cleaning up. She had enough problems on her hands trying to look after her frail husband. She often looked exhausted and depressed.

Jena did not understand this situation, especially where the elder couple was involved. They were no threat to anyone and yet were held as well. Their initial goal was to board another ferry from this island to the bigger island further south, which happened to be the island of Jena's birth. Jena and her siblings hoped to contact some relatives who would put them up when they got there. It was all they could afford. The plan was to send a telegram to their parents from there for enough money to get them home.

Every morning one policeman would show up at the inn and escort one of them to the station to be interrogated that day. They came for the older boys first and they were told not to tell anyone what happened at the station.

Suni was terrified, "What are they going to do to us Jena?" she cried. "What do I do when they take me? Jena I am scared!"

Jena did not know how to alleviate Suni's fears except to tell her not to be afraid, for they had done nothing wrong.

"Don't tell them anything, no matter what they threaten you with." Jena told her fiercely. "Keep saying the same thing over and over again, that you are just a teen trying to get home to your family."

And that was exactly what Jena did on the third day, when it was her turn to go. The officer walked her to the station without a word and then took her into a small empty room. There were three chairs and a table in it. A single light bulb provided the only light in the dark room. There were no windows. She was told to sit in one chair and two officers sat in the other ones across the table from her.

Jena thought that she would be petrified with fear by now and was amazed that she did not feel any apprehension at all. A strange calmness seemed to surround her all of a sudden and she felt as if she was outside of herself looking back at herself as an observer. She sensed many angelic spirits around her, especially Mary's loving presence, and heard her compassionate encouraging whispers swirl in her mind, "Be at ease, nothing will happen to you here. You are in the Mother's hands and you are safe. Answer the questions truthfully and all will be well. This will not last long."

One of them began the interrogation with accusations, "We believe that you are sent here to spy on us by the enemy of our country. You are rich Chinese children and you are pretending to be poor. We know that mostly Chinese Buddhists live in Singa. You are Chinese-born and they are your people and not our people, who are devout Muslims."

Jena kept repeating over and over again, "I am not a spy. I am only eighteen years old. We do not have much money, not even enough to get to Karta. I just want to go home to my parents. Please let us go. We have nothing to hide."

"What do you know about this war?" one of them insisted. "Why are you living in Singa?"

"I don't know anything about the war," Jena calmly replied. "I did not even know there was one. I am helping my widowed aunt. She does not have a girl child."

"Tell us, how many warships are there in the harbor?"

"I don't know anything about warships. I did not see them."

"You are lying! You live there. How could you not see the ships and not know that they are there? How many did you encounter when you crossed the border and where were they anchored?"

"We were smuggled out!" Jena cried in frustration. "We were kept hidden and could not see anything."

"Who smuggled you out, what is his name?"

"Hussein."

"Every other male Muslim man is called Hussein, what is his family name?"

"I don't know, he never told us."

"How was he able to get past the patrols of the warships?"

"I don't know."

The questioning went on and on. Jena lost track of how long she was kept there. She was surprised to notice that it was close to supper time when she was finally escorted back with the same command not to tell anything to anyone.

Jena immediately called a meeting and the five young adults met in the room that she shared with Suni. "We have to do something before they haul us back to the station again," Jena told them all. "We cannot sit here under indefinite house arrest and subject ourselves to such verbal abuse day after day. Besides, we don't have any money left to continue our journey if we stay much longer."

"The guard outside told me that they will come back for us again tomorrow," Hanli said. "I noticed that he is a chain smoker, so I slipped him some coffee money and hinted that we wouldl supply him with better quality cigarettes in exchange for information. He told me that the next time they would take all three of us Jena, you, Soto and myself. We'll have to make sure that we keep telling them the same story."

Fortunately, to everyone's grateful relief, they had not come for Suni and Johnnie, considering them to be too young to be questioned. They did not bother Mrs. Woo either when they found out that she did not speak the local language. Suni finally stopped crying and shaking when Jena told her not to worry about being hauled off to the station any longer.

The next morning was a repeat of the last questioning. The same deep calmness surrounded Jena as soon as she was seated before the interrogators. This time they kept asking her to describe the city and its surrounding area. Jena tried to accommodate them by telling them that she was just a schoolgirl who had no means of transportation and so did not know much about any kind of military installations. Apparently they asked Soto and Hanli the same questions when they were finally allowed to return to the inn.

Suni had been busy preparing the vegetables while Jena was at the station and waited anxiously for Jena to come back. Jena was therefore very busy cooking the evening meal upon returning and did not notice until dinner that Hanli was missing.

Johnnie volunteered to see if he was talking to the guard but only saw the guard sitting on a stool outside the gate having his own dinner. There was no sign of Hanli anywhere.

They waited in the courtyard outside their rooms anxiously. Nobody wanted to go to bed. Finally they heard him come in around midnight. They rushed up to him as Jena voiced their concerns, "Hanli, where have you been? You did not join us for mealtime and we were very worried that something had happened to you. I was afraid that they might have taken you back to the station for more questioning!"

"I snuck out," Hanli told them. "It's all right. I slipped the guard outside more coffee money and told him that I needed to buy some cigarettes or I would go crazy. Being the smoker that he is, I was hoping that he would be sympathetic to a fellow smoker and he fell for it," Hanli said smugly.

"Why didn't you tell us?" Jena asked with exasperation.

"You don't smoke!" Johnnie piped up in puzzlement.

"Well I pretended Johnnie," Hanli grinned, "I was not sure if I could bribe him to let me go or not and when he did, I left quickly before he could change his mind."

"You were gone for a long time, where did you go?" Soto asked.

"When I was let out of the interrogation room the other day, one of the officers secretly slipped me a piece of paper with an address on it. I was suspicious at first but I asked the innkeeper's wife if she knew where this address was. She told me that it was in the part of the town where most of the Chinese lived and that's where I went."

"The Chinese family who lived there told me that the man who slipped me the paper was half Chinese. He was a product of a rare interracial marriage and was able to become a police officer because he did not have the prominent Chinese features. Because of his position, he was able to help many people from the Chinese community and had told the community of the trouble we were in.

Officer Rito came in as I was talking with Mr. Ing, the man of the house. Rito was in civilian clothes and wore different glasses and I almost did not recognize him. He is willing to help us and here is what he suggests we do."

"All they want is money really," he told me. "These guys don't really care about the war. It is a big game to them. They follow the orders that come from the big city headquarters whenever it pleases them. They don't care if you are spies or not. However they do believe that you are rich kids and that you brought a lot of cash with you when you fled Singa. Everyone here knows that Singa is full of rich Chinese merchants and they want some of that abundance.

We have collected a donation from the community here to help you. Give me whatever amount you can spare and I will negotiate for you. I am pretty good at making up stories by now. I know how to play into their greed for they are actually good simple village men who only want a better life. Pay as a policeman is not sufficient to live on in this community. Every officer and government official in this town relies on bribes to supplement his income."

Then Mr. Ing gave me the following information, "The big ferry will arrive here in two days and you had better be sailing out with her for she won't be back for another two weeks after that. You don't want to be stuck here for that long. We cannot support you for that length of time. With the money collected from the community we have already purchased your ferry tickets for you. Bring all the money you can spare tomorrow when you are brought back to the station. Rito will help you further there as he promised."

"I thanked them for the tickets and for helping us then I got back as quickly as I could. The guard casually waved me through as I presented him with more cigarettes."

"I will go and talk to Mr. and Mrs. Woo," Jena volunteered. "I'll collect all the money we can spare and get it to you tonight. Thank you Hanli, that was really brave of you to go and have that secret meeting. Please tell Mr. Ing that we are very grateful and to thank the Chinese community for us. I wish I could thank them myself."

Early the next morning, Mrs. Woo was much relieved when Jena told her what happened and she gave Jena some money for the coffee money fund right away, "I am so glad that you young people are looking after us Jena. I was so worried when my daughter told me that we had to be smuggled home because we did not have the money for airfare either. My husband insisted on seeing his daughter one more time because he knows that he is dying. I did not want him to make the trip but Mimi my daughter wanted us to come to Singa because there are better medical facilities there. I knew that it was too late but Mimi did not want to hear that her father is dying. It was such a blessing when Hanli offered to help us."

"Start packing today," Jena suggested. "We have to be ready very early tomorrow morning and cannot afford to delay."

After breakfast, Officer Rito showed up to escort Jena, Hanli and Soto to the station one more time. "Play the game, indulge them," he instructed. "The station has to save face so that the other stations will not make fun of them. They pride themselves on having a successful interrogation program when they subject their victims to it for three days. This is your third day, don't aggravate them. Hanli, you will be their main target because they know that you have the coffee money with you. I will be in your room this morning. Wait for my signal before you begin offering the coffee money. Soto, just give the same answers you gave them for the past two days. Jena, you are a girl. In a Muslim society, girls are only good for marriage or as whores. Pretend to be just what they expect of you, a stupid spoiled girl, and don't deviate from the answers you gave them before."

The same calmness wrapped itself around Jena as she sat in the single chair waiting for the drama to unfold. As soon as they started to raise their voices, she began to whimper and cry. "I don't know, I don't know," became her mantra that morning. A couple of times one of them would slap the table top very loudly before her and scream in her face. Jena would cringe back in her seat pretending to be fearful and then increased her whimpering and moaning. After a while she even began to enjoy the whole charade and had a hard time not to giggle. She had to keep her hands over her eyes and her face to keep up the illusion of crying and moaning in terror. She could barely fathom the fact that she was not scared at all. That calmness and feeling of protection was like a solid rock around her.

It was a much happier and relieved trio who came out of the station late in the afternoon that day. Hanli had good news to share with the group once they were back at the Inn.

"It's all set," he told them. "I gave Rito the coffee money when he pretended to make a deal with me. That was his signal. He took the money to the captain's office and the captain agreed to let us board the ship tomorrow if I signed a statement to say that we are not spies and that we would not come back to this island. I agreed immediately and they allowed me to sign for all of us. Rito has somehow managed to be chosen as our escort tomorrow morning and will take us to the harbor at sunrise."

They were all packed and ready the next morning. Jena looked around her for the last time. It seemed such a beautiful island paradise but there was no peace here. An uneasy atmosphere of suspicion and distrust was boiling below the surface of this community and it created a pall of fear and discomfort. The group was very eager to leave this unhappy place at last.

Rito drove them in the police van to the harbor and took them aboard immediately. Because of his presence, they were waved through all the checkpoints. Jena suspected that there was coffee money being shared with all the officials at the harbor that morning.

"Sit down in your seats. Try to stay out of sight and don't talk to anyone," he warned them. Then he turned around and walked away without turning back.

The group of travelers was thankful beyond measure when the ferry slipped away from the dock and headed towards the open sea. It was a slightly bigger boat this time and it seated about fifty people. It was a longer ride and the captain told them that it would take at least eight hours before they would reach the harbor in Pankal.

To Jena's surprise, Mrs. Woo struck up a conversation with her during the long trip and shared with her that she knew Jena's family.

"My sister lives with her husband in Sungai and knew your grandmother quite well when she was alive. Your grandmother was well known as a healer and was well respected by the village. We were very sad when she died. My sister's son was very ill one day and it was your grandmother who healed him with her herbs. On the other hand, we do not like your grandfather Bune. He is a hard man and did not help the community when he could have. I hear that he has lost most of his business interests on the island. One of his sons, he would be your uncle I suppose, is looking after what is left of the family business."

Jena was delighted with the fact that Mrs. Woo had known her grandmother. What an opportunity this was! She immediately bombarded Mrs. Woo with a deluge of questions and begged her to tell her everything she knew about Singai. Mrs. Woo even knew grandmother's friend, the midwife, and told Jena how some people were afraid of Lowe.

"Some people are afraid of dukuns, Jena. They think that they are all black witches who deal with black magic. I know that Apho is a good person and would never befriend someone who deals in black magic. You should go and visit Sungai," she suggested.

"I intend to," Jena answered.

"Where are you staying in Pankal? I am afraid that with Mr.Woo being such a sick man I cannot invite you to my humble house in Pankal," Mrs. Woo apologized regretfully.

"We have some acquaintances there. I hope that they will take pity on us and put us up for a few days until we can board the big ferry to Karta."

"She is coming home to the island, Lowe," Apho whispered excitedly. *"How I wish that you and I were still there. What a homecoming that would be!"*

"We can still provide her with one," Lowe smiled. *"We can smooth her path for her and make sure that all goes well while she is on the island."*

"She needs to close this chapter of her life completely. We both know that she will soon leave this country never to return. She must leave everything that she has ever known in her life and close this first book."

Chapter Nine

Pankal was a busy harbor compared to the one they had departed from and there was the usual noisy confusion of a ship's arrival. Jena felt as if a heavy burden was at last taken from her shoulders when she realized that there were no policemen waiting for them at the wharf.

The group dispersed as soon as they disembarked from the ferry. For the last time, Mr.Woo was carried to a waiting taxi and Mrs. Woo climbed in after him after a quick goodbye to all of them. Hanli was next to leave. He had some business associates in town and would be making his way home with their assistance. Soto followed suit. He received a telegram from his family just before they left and his parents had sent him a plane ticket home from Pankal. He said his goodbyes just as speedily, promising to write when he got home to Banda, his home town. Jena knew that she would never see any one of them again, the same way she realized that she would never again see Aunt Liamay or Saria. There was a vague awareness as if doors were closing in the drama of her life. She noted what an odd sensation it was.

The three of them were left standing by themselves and knew that they were on their own for the final part of their journey. It was fortunate that Pankal was not a very big town and the taxi driver knew the location of the address that Jena showed him. They arrived at their destination unannounced again, and Jena hoped that Auntie Alib would take them in. Auntie Alib was not really an aunt to them for she was connected to the Bune's family by marriage. Every married lady, whether you were related to her or not, was addressed as 'Auntie' in the Chinese community and all adult men were called 'Uncle". It was a form of showing respect to your elders. Auntie Alib's sister was the lady who married Kosen. Soawie, Kosen's wife, had given Jena the address of her sister before Jena left for Singa.

"Who knows, Jena," Soawie said. "You have always wanted to go back and visit the island. If you do, my sister Alib has given you an open invitation to stay with her."

Soawie was true to her words because Alib welcomed them into her home right away. "I heard all about you from Soawie," Auntie Alib said. "Everyone is worried in Karta for no one knows what is happening with you. When the borders were closed, communication with Singa was not possible. Soawie guessed that you might try to reach Pankal and warned me of the possibility of your arrival. Stay as long as you wish, Jena, you are welcome in my home. I do have a favor to ask of you when you leave. Could you take my youngest son, Chenli, to

Karta? I want him to go to school there. My brother has offered to put him up and look after him there. Soawie has her own son to look after and besides, she has no room in her small home."

"Of course, I will Auntie," Jena promised.

The first priority was to send a telegram home telling her parents where they were and asking for funds to be sent to Alib's home. After that, there was really nothing they could do but wait.

It was the perfect time to do some exploring of the island and Jena told Alib what their plans were. "We would like to visit my grandmother's home in Sungai while we are here, Auntie. Which bus do I take?" Jena asked her.

It was not much of a bus. It was more a rickety old van packed with passengers. It took at least four hours of hazardous driving to get to the other side of the island where the village of Sungai was situated.

Jena knew that she was born here and that she had spent the first four years of her life here with Apho, Joan and Charlie. It was not what she expected and strangely she did not feel connected to anything in the village. As they walked around she had a sense of saying goodbye to something she was not quite sure of. They asked around and were directed to a small residential section where they found her grandmother's home. It was a nice home compared to some of the other small houses that they had seen in the village. The lady who owned the house was very gracious when they told her who they were and offered to show them around.

"My family knows your family. It is a small village you know, and everyone knows everyone's business here," she chuckled. "There was a lot of talk about the three of you arriving on the island. It was the most exciting news this village has enjoyed for a long time. We loved your grandmother and we still talk about all the work she did for the community."

"Things have really changed around here," Jena thought sadly. "This will be the last time I will ever see this place. I feel as if I have lost the story of my happy childhood here."

The lady knew where Grandfather Bune lived and directed them back to the village center. They thanked her for allowing them to see the garden and the house itself. When she found out that they had no place to stay, she told them that they could come back and sleep on the covered porch.

Uncle Kimly knew straight away who they were. You must be Kin's children," he said as he opened the door. "I heard that you were on the morning bus from Pankal." Grandfather was home that day and their uncle Kimli ushered them into the inner patio where he was sitting.

"We came to see Grandfather Bune, Uncle," Jena said politely. "We won't stay long."

There was no smiling welcome here. As a matter of fact it was uncomfortably hostile and all three visitors did not know what to make of it.

They were ushered before an old man sitting feebly in a rocking chair facing the inner courtyard of the house.

"We have some visitor's, Father. These are your grandchildren. They are Kin's youngsters."

Jena instantly felt sorry for her grandfather and looked at him with pity and compassion. She compared him to a pathetic, wrinkled old beggar she once saw sitting beside the road. She could only feel sad that his life would end in such a lonely and unloved manner. She forgave him for not acknowledging her and loving her as his granddaughter.

Grandfather seemed ill and feeble physically but his mind was surprisingly still very alert. "I have never met them, have I Kimli?" he asked his son as he peered at them with failing eyes.

"No father you have not."

"Are you sure that they are Kin's offspring?" he asked doubtfully.

"Oh I am sure, Father. Just look at the boy. He looks just like Kin when he was that age."

"By the ancestors, you are right. Come here boy and let me look at you," he commanded Johnnie.

Johnnie came dutifully forward and politely shook his grandfather's hand. Jena and Suni were only granted a casual glance. Grandfather Bune had no use for girls and treated his own daughters abominably.

It was a very brief visit but obviously one that made an impact on the old man.

"Kimli, give the children some pocket money," he ordered his son when they rose to say goodbye. That was an unusual request and it startled their uncle as he turned his eyes to them. Jena felt his animosity as soon as she caught his unguarded look of intense dislike directed towards the three of them.

"He's afraid that we'll try to get money out of the old man," Jena thought.

It was no surprise that Kimli ignored his father's wish and escorted them out of the house. Without a word of goodbye, he closed the door firmly behind them.

Much later, Jena came to the knowledge that Kimli had taken over the running of whatever business the family still owned and had pocketed all the profits himself.

The three siblings drove back to Pankal quietly the next day. Each had their own thoughts about the strange visit.

Auntie Alib asked them how the visit went when they got back and they all agreed that it was a good trip. It was good that they had finally met their grandfather and it was good that they saw what the village of Sungai looked like.

For Suni and Johnnie, that was all it was because Suni was a very tiny baby when she left. For Johnnie, it was an adventure because he was not born in Sungai and was too young to understand the strained relationship between his mother's and father's families.

For Jena, it was a different matter and she felt the same strange feeling of old invisible strands being detached from her as she looked up at the stars in the sky that night.

"In my human form I have hated that man." Apho confessed. *"Now all I can see is what a hefty karmic price he has paid for his ignorance and his emotional abuse towards his wife and his daughters."*

"Free will is a wonderful gift but what a sharp two-edged sword it is. The Earth lessons are the hardest and most challenging ones in the whole Universe, my friend. It cannot be learned in just one lifetime. Human lives are so short and that is why we choose to reincarnate over and over again until hopefully we master each one. Sometimes it takes many lifetimes just to learn one lesson, especially the more difficult ones like forgiveness."

"I am glad then, that I forgave him before I died," Apho's spirit said gratefully. *"Thank you for your help, dear friend. Without your gentle teachings, I would have to carry that karmic debt into my next life and I really do not wish to go through that painful experience again."*

"You did all the work yourself, Old One. My job was only to give the information you needed and you made your own choice based on your acceptance of the lesson. There are so many human souls out there who have not made that choice even though they have received the information like you did."

"I am glad that the children were able to face him with their innocence. Jena at least has been given the opportunity to see with her own eyes where her father's character originated from. She is old enough to have heard many of Lian's bitter renditions of the old family feud stories between the Liu and the Bune clans."

"Your gentle guidance paid off Apho. Did you notice the wonderful beam of light that emanated from her heart

the moment she forgave him?" Lowe's spirit glowed with happiness as she peered into the mirror-like surface of the crystal.

Chapter Ten

It took ten days for the money to arrive and the group of four now prepared for their departure on another ferry boat. There was not enough money for airfare, but enough to buy the cheapest tickets possible for passage on the ferry. They had decided to buy the cheapest fare so that they had enough money left over in case of emergencies. All of them had no idea what space a cheap ticket would buy and neither did Auntie Alib for she had always flown to Karta.

They therefore had no idea what to expect when it was time for departure. The boat was much larger than the one that brought them to the island. It was more like a ship that had cabins on the upper deck and an empty arena-like room below. To their horror, this was where they were shoved and pushed by a frenzied crowd. Everyone with the same tickets as theirs was herded towards the bowels of the ship when the entrance gate was opened. It was a race to claim a tiny floor space in this cavernous hole. There were at least two hundred people, almost piled on top of each other, along with their luggage. They all had to share this confining space.

They finally found a tiny corner, and huddled miserably on top of their suitcases. There was no adequate space left for them by the time they realized what was happening. Jena could barely breathe. There were no windows and the stench of unwashed human bodies on top of the smell of the inadequate toilet facilities was nauseating. This time it was an overnight voyage, for they would not arrive in Karta until the next morning.

The thought of spending the night in this hole of human misery was too much for Jena. It was unbearable, and it was suffocating for her. To top it all off they were told that there were groups of thieves roaming the area, stealing from the sleeping unsuspecting passengers. The lady on the floor beside them told her that they were already targeted because of their youth. Jena left Suni and Chenli to guard their belongings while she and Johnnie tried to find a solution on the upper deck.

There were people sleeping everywhere on the upper decks as well. Carefully, they stepped over slumbering bodies as they made their way to the door that would lead to the enclosed area where the cabins were. They finally cornered a steward and began to negotiate the possibility for a small cabin. By the time they bribed the steward to give them a room and then pay for the room itself, they had barely any money left for food. Jena did not care at that point. She had to get everyone in her group out of the bowels of the ship!

Gratefully, the four of them gathered all their belongings and carried them into the narrow cabin. The cabin had only one bed and a tiny toilet. A private toilet was considered a luxury beyond the imagination for the majority of the passengers traveling that day. They decided to take turns sleeping on the bed and the rest would sleep on the floor. Jena could barely remember sleeping that night. In one moment she was happy to get home, but the next minute she was apprehensive about the reception that awaited her. Will her mother be very angry at her for not spending the money as wisely as she could? Would they be angry at her for not looking after her brother and sister properly? Would they blame her for the failed attempt at leaving the country?

From what Auntie Alib told her, the unrest in Karta had not lessened and was causing major worries for the Chinese community. The rich Chinese merchants were already evacuating their families to other countries. The middle class groups were scrambling to find foreign countries that would take them in. Those with grown children, especially girls, sent them out immediately to Europe or the United Sates of America, depending on how much a family could afford.

It was dawn when they heard the commotion of the docking procedures. They did not have any money left to buy breakfast and it did not take them long to gather their cases and join the long line that was waiting for the signal to disembark.

The noise and the chaos in the big harbor were overwhelming as Jena looked down from the ship's deck towards the quay. There were people everywhere going to and fro, milling here and there. It reminded Jena of a group of ants looking for hidden food. Nobody seemed to know where they were going! How on earth were they to find their family? Jena fervently hoped that her mother had received the letter she had written telling the time and day of their arrival.

Finally they walked down the gangway and that was when they saw their mother and Charlie, their older brother. They were standing beside another man. Charlie was waving and yelling their names, trying to get their attention.

The man was a valuable ally who would help them traverse the busy turmoil of the harbor. Mother introduced him as Uncle Soba. Uncle Soba knew all the harbor officials and was an expert in getting his way using the coffee money method. He worked for an export company and the harbor was his daily work environment. With his help they were soon driving home in the family car. Jena did not recognize the car. They must have bought a new one while she was away in Singa.

It felt so odd to be going back to the home she had left more than three years ago. Everything felt different and looked strange. Her mother's behavior towards her was peculiar as soon as they met. It was as if it was a different person who greeted her at the harbor.

Auntie Jan was still there and welcomed them happily. Chenli's family was waiting for him and gratefully whisked him away.

Those first few days were filled with explanations and the exchange of stories. The family wanted to know where they had been, and how they made it home. Then they were informed of all the changes that had happened to the family within those three years.

There was some sad news as well, especially for Jena, when Joan gently told her that Kosen had passed away. It was another sense of closure for Jena as she grieved for him. As the days went by there was more unsettling news to share. The family had not given up the idea of relocation, especially since it was getting more and more dangerous for Chinese-born citizens.

Kin, their father, was fortunately able to hold on to his managerial position in a company that wanted exposure to the markets in the West. He was the one who was able to become their contact because of his knowledge of the English language. His boss was very happy with the new trade routes now open to him and was very indulgent of Kin's eccentric behavior. Kin understood that there was no future for his children in this country any longer. A good life here was unattainable because of their Chinese heritage. He was able to save enough money and at the same time could procure a loan from his boss to finance the departure of only Joan and Luan to Germany. It was the only country that was willing to give out two year working permits to foreign applicants. The sisters had to work for their own living expenses and could not afford to go to a country that would not allow them to earn a living.

Jena was devastated and livid at the news that she could not go too. Here she was home at last but what a homecoming it was. Her cousin Greta, who was in the same class she attended before she left for Singa, had recently graduated from the convent school and was now entering University. It hit Jena hard and she felt as if a storm was brewing inside of her. As she watched the excitement of her sisters' departure, the storm within became a hurricane, with a tornado close behind it. She felt cheated, victimized, betrayed, a complete failure and utterly unloved.

"I want to go too," she angrily confronted her mother. "I want to get out of this country now! You have caused the three of us three years of misery. We lost our education when you sent us to Singa. How could you send us without writing to your own sister first and asking her if she was in agreement with your plans? Did you not know how she hates us all?"

Jena did not care what her mother's reaction would be to her anger and she would not back down in her demands of compensation for the lost years. She stood there defiantly with eyes flaming, her long black unruly hair whipped across her face as she shook with fury. She expected her mother to take out the whip again but, to her bewilderment, her mother bowed her head in shame and remorse.

"I am so sorry, Jena," she mumbled sadly. "We made a big mistake sending the three of you to your aunt. I don't blame you for being so angry. I promise that we'll do whatever is necessary to make it up to you. But you cannot go with your sisters, we do not have the money to send three of you."

Jena was amazed at the change in her mother's attitude towards her and felt a shift in their relationship to a more positive level of communication. Her mother was definitely not the same person she knew three years ago. "Perhaps I am seeing her in a more mature manner," Jena thought to herself. "After all, three years is a long time and I am a lot older now. She is my mother and she cannot help it that Grandma spoiled her so."

"You cannot go yet, Jena," Joan tried to console her. "You must get your high school certificate first or you will not get a good job in Germany. We will send money home when we get there and as soon as you have your papers, we'll send for you. Start learning the German language now. The German embassy has opened its doors and offers language classes because there are so many young Chinese students who have applied for visas."

Jena was still very unhappy with the solution but accepted the final argument because she knew that it cost a lot of money to leave the country now. The government had created special taxes when it was known that there was an exodus of young Chinese students. Besides the taxes, there were large amounts of bribes required at every exit point. Whether it was the airport or the harbor, the word was passed around among the officials, and they were gleefully ready to pounce upon this windfall.

"I want tutors," Jena demanded next, "tutors in every subject I am behind in, and I want to enter the finals in one year and not three."

"All right, Jena," her mother sighed with resignation. "I will inform your father to set aside some money for you."

"We will try to send you all away as soon as we can," Lian the mother informed them. "Just remember that we can only provide you with a one-way ticket. You must find your own way out there in that foreign land. We cannot help you financially once you get there and you cannot come back home again."

"Who in their right mind would want to come back to this inhospitable country?" Jena thought to herself.

To add insult to injury, the war that was the cause of such a horrendous journey for the three younger Bune children ended as suddenly as it began. The borders were reopened and the first news that came through was about Auntie Liamay's death. At least her son arrived in time to say goodbye to his mother before she passed away at home. It was not an easy transition apparently. Liamay was in excruciating pain and suffered until her last breath. Jena grieved for her aunt and felt deep compassion and sorrow that she had to endure so much in her life.

"What an extraordinary coincidence that such a flash war happened just when I needed an escape route!" Jena marveled at this seeming evidence of Divine intervention. As far as she was concerned, her sense of deep gratitude to the Holy Mother would continue for the rest of her life. That deep calmness and sense of protection would sustain her in every crisis she had yet to face.

Joan and Luan left not long after Jena's arrival. The first letters that came from Germany were not very informative at first. Both girls left with only an address of a daughter of one of Lian's acquaintances from the beauty school. They had no idea if the girl even knew that they were coming. It was a frightening and worrisome voyage for both girls and they were very thankful when they met two other sisters on the ship. The two sisters had already established jobs in another German city and offered to help the Bune sisters. It was a god-send as they followed their new friends to the north, where they were able to find jobs within days of their arrival.

Within months, Joan and Luan sent money home and it was enough to finance the departure of Charlie who had his high school certificate already.

Jena's determination was now the engine that drove her relentlessly towards her goal. "One year," she promised herself. "One full year and I want out of here!"

True to their word, her parents gave her the money and Jena hired the tutors that she needed. At first, she tried to get back into her former school the convent school for girls. She was deeply saddened and hurt when Mother Superior, the principal refused her entry. She was too old, the nun told her and too far behind. She would have to start all over again and complete the three year program like everyone else.

One bright light amidst all the challenges however was the pleasant revelation in regards to the Church situation. Her parents had relented and had even allowed Joan and Luan to be baptized into the Catholic Church before they left. Suni did not wish to be the odd man out and asked to be baptized too. There was of course an obvious incentive to do so, when her mother realized that most of the girls who were able to leave the country were Catholics. The Church, it appeared, had quietly begun to help anyone who was a Catholic to leave the country quickly. Congregations in Europe were donating funds for this purpose. The nuns were secretly helping the girls at the convent with this.

It was a gamble Lian was willing to take, but it did not work. Unfortunately the Bune sisters did not try to develop a close relationship with the nuns and were not chosen for this program. According to the one nun who was sympathetic to their cause, the sisters were too poor, too quiet, too weak in their commitment to the church and just too odd.

Jena was amused when she found out and at the same time regretted the fact that her joining the Church had exacted such a very high price. However, there was never a moment of doubt in her mind that she had made the right choice in becoming a part of Mary's family.

She continued her close relationship with Mary, even though her own mother's manner towards her had mellowed into a kind of acceptance. Jena believed that it must be Divine intervention that caused her to find a private school very quickly. This school catered to the children of the rich Chinese community who were also behind in their studies because they had been schooled overseas. It was the perfect solution to her plans.

Suni and Johnnie followed suit and also asked to be enrolled in the same school. Both were young enough that they could still enter their age appropriate levels. Jena insisted that they also receive help until they caught up with their peers. With Joan, Luan and Charlie gone, there was enough money to pay for all the special classes the three of them needed.

It became a marathon for Jena as she began to study day and night. Black coffee became her bosom friend during this time period. It was a race against the clock. She had missed so much and was so far behind that she was often in despair for, at the same time, she also had to attend a language class at the German embassy to prepare for her voyage to that country. Yet somehow whenever she hit those low points, there was always Mary's gentle voice guiding her back towards sanity.

It took more than one year in the end, because the final exams took place in mid-year. It gave Jena more time and she was extremely grateful for it. Her math and science teacher often shook his head telling her that she was crazy to cram so much into eighteen months. "You'll never make it, Jena," he told her at every tutoring session. "You are lacking three years of instruction!"

Jena was very persistent and insistent that he continue to tutor her for the exam. "You know what they will be asking at these exams," Jena begged him. "Teach me the questions that have appeared in previous exams and forget about teaching me what I've missed by grade levels. I can do it, I can!"

The final exam was a state exam. Every high school student had to write the same tests on the same day throughout the country. Every school would compete to produce the one student who would receive the highest marks. The most coveted ones were the ones in Mathematics and Science. It would enhance the school's ratings. For years, it was always the convent school that would walk away with the largest number of students achieving the highest marks in most subject areas.

The dreaded day came and Jena sat nervously in the huge hall where the exams were being held. They were constantly supervised by teachers of different schools. It took one week to write the exam for every subject. Jena's head was reeling by the end of the week and when her mother asked her how it went she could only shake her head. "I don't know," she moaned. "I don't remember how I got through any of it."

Then came the waiting and waiting. To prevent herself from going crazy, Jena began her preparations for her departure without delay. She persuaded one of her cousins to give her a ride on his motorbike to the passport office and waited patiently for days to be allowed to fill in an application form. After carefully slipping large amounts of coffee money into some receptive palms, she was able to complete the forms with the promise that she would have her documents soon.

Auntie Jan tried to help her as well and suggested that Jena accompany her in a cross-island trip. Again Jena was taken aback when her mother agreed to pay for the trip. She could barely recognize this person who was trying so hard to be a more loving mother to her. Jena came to the conclusion that her mother must be missing Luan in a big way or was truly trying to repair their relationship. Whatever it was, Jena decided to take advantage of her good fortune and gratefully accepted Auntie Jan's offer. It would take three weeks and when they got back the exam results should be posted by then.

It was an escorted trip in a small tour bus that would take them all the way to the island of Bali. The population of Bali was unique in that they were all Hindus and followed the ancient Hindu teachings. They were a gentle friendly people and their intricate temple dances were fascinating. Jena was so taken with it, that when she returned home and heard that a Balinese dance master was in town she and Suni enrolled in a class.

It was a wonderful opportunity for Jena to visit this remarkable island, especially since she knew that she would never see these wonderful sights again.

"Finally, finally I see that Lian has accepted this child just the way she is," the proud grandmotherly spirit smiled. "Lian still does not understand Ayin and never will but at least she is willing to accept and tolerate her own daughter."

"Don't forget that Lian is getting older as well, Old Friend. With age comes wisdom, remember? She is remorseful and wants desperately to be accepted by her daughter. She misses Luan and is beginning to listen to other people's voices when they tell her how engaging and smart Jena is."

"Look into her heart," Lowe's spirit continued as she peered deeper into the scrying surface. "This granddaughter of yours is spiritually rising by leaps and bounds. She has already begun to forgive her mother and is accepting her the way she is. Ayin understands that her mother is one of those childlike adults who chose not to mature in her life-time. Now this is just the first layer. The deeper layers of forgiveness will require more maturity and spiritual awareness on Ayin's part."

"I am so happy to see that some of my lessons have surfaced within her consciousness Lowe," Apho joined in. Then she chuckled as she spied something else in the mirroring depths, "Did you notice how many scholarly spirits were helping her as she studied for this demanding exam? I am especially in awe of that old monk who kept peering over her shoulder."

"That old monk, my friend, was a well-known mathematician on the earth plane many years ago and has offered to help Jena. You and I are no good at that mathematical stuff, are we?" Lowe admitted as she joined in her friend's amusement.

"This trip is a gift for her, she has earned it and the memories of it will provide her with enjoyment and peace," Lowe continued. 'It will give her the knowledge and awareness of the Hindu religion, giving her another tool for her spiritual toolbox. Finally this is a closing goodbye, for this lotus seedling is about to breach the surface of her existence and face a new dawn.

Chapter Eleven

It was a journey of discovery for Jena and a much needed vacation after the exhausting year she had had. The rickety old bus was filled with seniors and Jena was amused to find that she was the centre of attention. She became the token granddaughter of the whole group.

She was overcome by the beauty of the land they were visiting and by the villagers they met. Jena found them very friendly and no one cared that the visitors were all of Chinese descent. Everywhere they stopped they were met with smiles and polite greetings of welcome.

One of their destinations was an old Hindu temple in the centre of a tiny Hindu kingdom. Jena was ecstatic to discover the existence of this tiny kingdom hidden in this vast Muslim country. She felt as if she was transported into one of her favorite fantasy novels. The temples astounded her as she explored their inner chambers. The ancient stone structures were covered with intricate carvings of strange depictions of gods and goddesses. Jena sensed the presence of great power here and was at first alarmed by it until she realized that it was just her own ignorance of the unknown that caused the fear. She tried to listen more attentively to the narration of the guides as they led the group into the temple's compound.

It was a disappointment for the group when the guide apologetically announced that they were not allowed into the palace as the Sultan was in residence that week.

The second week found them entering Surabaya, the city where Jena lived for a few years. She persuaded Auntie Jan to accompany her for a visit to the old neighborhood and to her delight found that her childhood friend Hildi was still living in the same house. She remembered her childhood promise to Hildi that she would return one day and this was it.

It was an odd visit. Hildi was extremely shy and Jena barely recognized her. Of course it had been more than ten years since they saw each other and there had been no communication during those years. Hildi and her family looked upon her in awe. In their eyes she had grown into a sophisticated, very assured young lady. For Jena, it was as if she was meeting a group of strangers whose lives were stuck in the past for they had not changed at all. Sadly, she bade the family goodbye knowing that this was another door to be closed permanently. She did not belong here any more.

A few days later they boarded a ferryboat and crossed the narrow strait that separated Bali from the mainland. Jena could not help but compare this trip to the other ferries she had been on. What a gift this crossing was, for now she could truly enjoy every moment of it without any worry. The deep blue of the ocean waters surrounded the boat on all sides and Jena gratefully breathed in the cleansing, clear, salty air as she leant over the railing. The sky was clear and the bluest she had ever seen. The golden rays of the sun permeated every particle of air and Jena enjoyed its warm embrace. Once again an intense sensation shivered within her and Jena felt her eyes tearing as she acknowledged the absolute beauty of this vista. With a shock, she recognized the feeling as the energy of Love and she understood that this was what Divine Love must feel like.

"How can anyone not thank the Creator for this wonderful world we live in?" she wondered. "And how can some people refuse to believe that there is a God who created all this beauty?"

Bali was a captivating place. It had a very different atmosphere. The people were such gentle and friendly souls. Their Hindu-based belief system was evident everywhere. Numerous altars dotted the roadsides and each was supplied with brilliant freshly picked flowers every day. Sacred temples were in every town or village and sacred services were held daily. The people were devoted to the Divine here and lived their daily lives accordingly. They believed in the Oneness of things and honoring other religions was part of their understanding.

Jena was exuberant when she could attend one of the sacred ceremonies. Different temple dances accompanied by gamelan music was part of these ceremonies. She was enthralled by the dancers.

As she and Auntie Jan wandered around the city, they saw many other wonderful sights. The women wore brilliant blooms in their hair as they walked with their wares balanced on their head to a temple or to the market. The people were poor materially but Jena found no sadness here as she roamed the market place. She had brought some extra dresses and she bartered them for the famous wood carvings displayed all over the market. The daughter of the lady who managed the market stall was very grateful and happy when Jena gave her an extra dress as part of the deal. The girl told her that she had never seen such a beautiful dress in her life. Jena wished at that moment that she had brought more. She had acquired much materially since there was more money coming in for the family and her fervent wish was to be able to share more.

It was sad to leave this beautiful fairyland and Jena wished with all her heart that this island would maintain its pristine innocence in the future.

The journey home however was not an easy one for Jena. She became ill and it was soon obvious to the group that she was not getting better, in fact, she was getting worse. Everyone was worried and at last the whole bus agreed to return immediately, cutting the excursion short by a few days.

Jena was barely conscious by the time they got her home and her mother anxiously took her to a doctor right away. Good medical doctors were a rare find during those times and very expensive. It was fortunate that Lian, because of her brothers, knew the doctor who lived in the area personally. When she knocked on his door with a very sick daughter, the doctor worked on Jena at once as he realized how ill she was. He told Lian that it was a close call and it was an interesting coincidence that he happened to have some antibiotics at home that day.

It took weeks for Jena to recuperate and she was still very weak when the exam results came in. Her friend Tani, who was in the same class, came rushing in one day and shouted out her news in excitement, "Jena, we passed, we both passed! And guess what!! You won the highest mark in Math!"

Jena was stunned. It was beyond her wildest dreams. She made it, she did it!! It was now time to complete the preparations for her departure.

Her principal, Mrs. Tan, was very excited when Jena came to collect her papers. "Oh no, Jena," she said. "I don't have your certificate. You have earned the privilege of receiving your certificate from the president's daughter herself in a special ceremony next week. You are to present yourself and appear in native formal dress of course. I am so proud of you. Do you realize that this is the first time anyone from my school has won this honor?" Mrs Tan was beside herself with pride.

The whole family got involved in trying to get her ready. Jena had never worn the native sarong and kebaya and had to learn how to wind the sarong properly around her waist. A special lacy kebaya, the native blouse, had to be ordered and then she had to practise twisting her hair in the shape of a bun at the back of her head. It was the required hairdo for the outfit. Unfortunately, no one could go with her and she found herself being pedaled in a rickshaw to the appointed place. To her consternation and astonishment, she had a couple of men on bicycles following her rickshaw and taking turns addressing her, trying to get her attention. "Hey beautiful lady, where are you going? May I escort you? I would like to get to know you? Where do you live?"

She ignored them and the rickshaw driver finally told them to stop following him. "Me, they called me beautiful? It was amusing when two little boys in grade five thought I was pretty, but grown men? They must be blind or desperate!" Jena dismissed the whole incident. She had more important things to consider and to plan for her forthcoming departure.

"How proud you must be at this moment Apho," her friend smiled. *"She certainly inherited the intelligence from your side of the family. She has earned this short lived fame."*

"I hope that it won't go to her head," the proud grandmother answered.

"No need to worry, Old One. The Goddess has anchored her energy of love and compassion deep into this child. Her sense of honor will stabilize and strengthen her humility."

"What is that illness all about, Lowe? I don't quite understand the flow of things here."

"It is one of her exit points. You know as well as I that we have been given many opportunities to choose whether we wish to continue with this lifetime or not. Remember that day when I fell in the market? That was one for me. You had one too when you became ill after the children left. You were so despondent and depressed that you almost chose to leave the earth plane."

"Ayin is about to enter a very different world altogether and face diverse challenges. She was given a window and had to choose. We are very happy here that she chose to stay and continue her earthly journey. The illness had two functions as we see here. One was the choice of living and the other was an avenue for her body to release all the heavy congestion she had been carrying for so long. Her body is preparing to shoulder other frequencies of experiences."

"I am glad that she has decided to stay too," Apho commented. "Although it would have been a joyous occasion if she had chosen to come home, don't you think?"

Her friend chuckled, "You miss her, don't you?"

"I do and so do you! On the other subject matter, you must admit my friend that it was a humorous way to show her how pretty she is and to neutralize her mother's incessant harping on her daughter's so-called ugliness."

"We will continue to present many mirrors to her for she needs to enter into the understanding that all is beauty in the eyes of the Creator. The human lesson is to be able to see through the eyes of the Mother-Father God and accept everyone and everything as beautiful. It has been a hard lesson for Lian when four beautiful spirits chose her as a mother in this lifetime. Her earthly life would have taken a very different turn if she had realized how beautiful they were and what an honor they had bestowed upon her."

"We both know that it is time for Ayin to close the first book of her life. The memory of it will be the foundation of the wisdom that will be hers to harvest in later years. She has overcome all the hurdles that she had written into this first book of her earthly journey and has completed it well.

She will never have to face the trauma of her childhood years again and will have a life full of abundance from now on."

"*She will meet many different people for the two years of her stay in Germany. It will be a time of preparation for her, although she is not aware of it. She will be given the opportunity to mature and acclimatize herself in the white man's society. She will reach her final destination in two years and it will be a true homecoming for her, for she will recognize the land itself.*"

Chapter Twelve

Kin rarely communicated with his children and it was therefore a noteworthy occurrence when he addressed Jena one day. "I have procured a job for you with one of the German firms we are having business dealings with," he informed her. "You are to be an invoice typist in their international department in Germany. I suggest you take the appropriate classes to qualify for this job. Don't make a liar out of me because I told them that you are qualified."

The weeks before her departure were a frenzied time of preparations for Jena. Besides attending the German language classes, Jena also had to accelerate her secretarial classes in order to get all her papers on time.

It was also a difficult time for Suni because she would be left on her own without the support of her sister. Jena did her best to console her, "We'll send money back for you Suni. It won't be long. You'll graduate in two years and then you can join us in Germany. Keep dreaming and planning for what you want to be when you get there."

The dangerous unrest around them did not get any better and nobody talked to their neighbors any longer. The essence of Fear was thick everywhere. There was now a curfew in place in the city. The girls were warned not to travel by themselves and Jena had to be driven and picked up from all her classes. Johnnie, being the only son, now would bike to his classes but was also warned to be extremely careful. He was late one day. It was after six curfew time and his mother was getting frantic. He finally arrived home shaken and muddied.

"I had to get off my bike fast," he told them. "They started shooting in the city. I threw myself into a muddy ditch for bullets were flying over my head. One bullet almost hit me!" Everyone was very careful to obey the curfew times after that episode.

Disturbing news spread over the city like wildfire when a number of the generals were assassinated by their own army officers. Fear escalated. Riots exploded in the inner city. Bodies floated in the muddy waters of the city's canal. Chinese merchants fled as their stores and warehouses were burned. Anyone caught in Chinatown was tortured and killed.

It was physically painful for Jena when she heard that one of her classmates had been abducted. She was later found brutally raped and tortured. Jena had difficulty dealing with this violence and it strengthened her resolve never to return to this hostile environment. After this incident the Chinese community was scrambling to send their daughters away as soon as possible.

One of Luan's friends came to ask if she could travel with Jena. One of the nuns had found her a job as a nurse in the same city where Jena was going. Jena was glad of the company and the fact that she did not have to travel alone to a strange and foreign land. The two girls began to share all their travel preparations and Lili became a frequent visitor in the Bune's home. They practised their cooking skills together for they did not know what to expect when they arrived in their new home. Other survival skills were also explored, such as how to sew pleated skirts and what herbs to take in case of illness.

Lili had a rich aunt, and the aunt had agreed to finance her journey, with the idea that Lili then would help pay for her sister's departure as soon as she could.'

The money that Joan and Luan had sent was used for Charlie's departure and there was not enough to pay for Jena's ticket yet.

It was a trying time for Jena, especially when her mother told her that the officials had raised the taxes again. Exit permits to leave the country were at a premium and there were long line-ups of desperate people in front of the offices. It was a frustrating time and it required all the patience Jena could muster to deal with the delay. It seemed as if obstacle after obstacle was put in her way. She felt as if vicious vines were twisting and turning around her, trying to bind her and hold her back as she strained desperately to escape.

The price of coffee money rose to an unprecedented high as the officials would only process the required documents for those offering the highest amount. It did not matter that you were the first in line any longer. The official would casually ask you to move back as he traversed the desperate line waiting for the one who had the most coffee money to offer that day.

It was too dangerous for Jena to go on her own and Kin, her father, could not afford to stay away from his office too long. After standing in line with her for one whole day, he decided to hire someone to take her. Uncle Soba re-entered her life at that point and he took charge right away. He told her to sit down in a corner and remain there until he called her. "Leave everything to me," he said. "You are a girl and they will not deal with you. Don't say anything and don't do anything until I call you to sign the papers."

Jena happily agreed and within three days she was issued her exit permits and could then proceed to purchase a ticket on the next ship out. Uncle Soba had to do the negotiating for that too since it involved another set of coffee money exchanges.

In the meantime, Jena's wardrobe had to be adjusted as Joan's and Luan's letters warned her that she needed winter clothes. Not knowing what winter was all about, except that it involved snow and extreme cold, they had to make some guesses. Auntie Tin, whose daughter lived in Holland had just returned and gave Jena a pair of nylons. Jena thought that they were absolutely beautiful and carefully packed them in her suitcase.

"You must wear these when you are in the west among the white people Jena," Auntie Tin shared with her. "All the women wear them. It is part of the fashion over there." What Auntie failed to tell Jena was that you needed a girdle to attach the nylons to. Jena found them so delicate and fine that she did not want to ruin them by trying them on until she got aboard the ship. Both girls were puzzled when the nylons kept falling off their legs and could not understand how the other ladies kept them on. It was the first of many hilarious incidences as Jena learned to adjust to a whole new way of living.

Fortunately, Luan and Joan told her that they would pick her up at the train station on her arrival and bring her a winter coat and winter boots to wear. "It will be winter when you get here Jena," they wrote. "Be prepared for the cold and the snow."

Lili and Jena were both excited and could barely wait to feel the cold white snow for the first time in their lives. "Maybe we could eat it the way we enjoy shaved ice cones here," Jena suggested.

The much awaited day came at last and Jena could barely contain her excitement. Everyone in the family wanted to see her off that day and they all piled into two separate cars heading to the harbor. When they got there, Lili was already there with her family.

Uncle Soba was given the task once more of negotiating with the multiple harbor checkpoints. Jena was appalled months later when her mother informed her that Jena's exodus cost her family over a million rupias that day.

When it came time for a thorough screening by a lady customs officer, both girls were prepared because Uncle Soba had warned them beforehand. They had the required coffee money and some trinkets ready in hand. There was a pretense of a body search of course. While in the booth, Jena casually mentioned the coffee money envelope that she had in her palm, then invited the lady to confiscate the pretty necklace and earrings she had deliberately left on top of her small case. It worked and the lady official let her go without insisting that she take her clothes off.

Family members were not allowed in the entrance area and were all standing in the spectator section on the quay. Jena and Lili walked up the ramp into the ship and were awed at its size. It was a magnificent white cruise ship that happened to come for a short visit a couple of days before. The captain had not realized the extent of the troubles that were plaguing the city and wanted to get away speedily.

Lili and Jena stood on the upper deck where all the passengers were gathered to say goodbye to their families and friends below. Jena felt exhilarated as the white ship detached itself from the harbor and began to glide smoothly away. She waved and waved as long as she could. Finally, she could not see anyone clearly any longer. The ship sailed out of the harbor and headed into the open waters of the Indian Ocean.

Jena continued to stand on the deck for a very long time, long after most of the passengers had gone below to get ready for dinner. Lili decided to go down to their cabin as well and left Jena alone with her thoughts.

The setting sun bathed everything it touched with a red and orange glow. The ocean waters looked like Jena's favorite red papaya juice as it rippled in the warm evening breeze. It was a phenomenal sunset, a perfect setting for a last goodbye. "It is such a beautiful land," she mused. "What a shame that it is painted with the darkness of so much anger and violence. I have at last left this place of my birth and I know that I will never return. Everything

I have ever known in my life is disappearing before my eyes." Jena felt tears silently flowing down her cheeks. They were not tears of regret or of sadness. Instead, they were tears of goodbye for her old self and her childhood years.

She was heading into uncharted waters now. Everything from this moment on was an unknown. "What kind of life will I encounter?" she asked herself. "Will the people like me? Will I like them? Will they discriminate against me because of who I am? What rules do I have to follow? What are the customs and belief systems of these strange people? Even the weather patterns of the four seasons will be a new adventure for me."

The rug seemed to have been pulled from under her feet and it left her with a strange uncomfortable feeling in her stomach. She was very happy to leave, and yet, facing the unknown was very intimidating at the same time.

The sun had disappeared below the far horizon and the stars were becoming more visible in the darkening sky. Jena sighed deeply and fleetingly wondered what her grandmother would think of it all. She turned her back symbolically and stood for a silent moment facing the stairwell, staring down into the lower deck, down into the unknown, down into the doorway of a new beginning.

"All lines to her old life have been severed now, Lowe," the grandmother spirit sighed. "She felt me there for one eternal second and thought about me, did you see that? How I wished I could gather her in my arms again at that moment."

"Yes, I witnessed that precious moment, Old Friend," Lowe smiled lovingly. "You know of course that it is now time for me to leave you."

"Yes, old partner," Apho returned the loving smile. "I shall miss you dearly. Have you decided where you will be headed?"

"My assignment, as enjoyable as it was working with you, has been completed and I must move on. I have reached the levels required to move into the higher dimensions and will be working with others of like interests there. We will meet again, Old Healer. We both know that there is no real separation within the Oneness."

"It is wonderful that you have chosen to continue to be a guide for Ayin until she wakes up. She needs you and is familiar with your vibration. Great things await this grandchild of yours Apho. As we both saw in the crystal, she will not stay long in this country called Germany. It is only a way-station for her, a launching pad so to speak. She will at last experience moments of happiness and joy there and it will prepare her for her life in the new world."

"Thank you for your support Lowe. She does not need such close supervision anymore now. Her regular angelic guides will take over and I will only be here occasionally to see how she is doing. I have chosen to continue my interests in this layer until her time of awakening."

"The Lotus child is growing up my friend and will soon be transplanted permanently to the proper environment for her. She will fly across another ocean within two years with an expanded set of spiritual tools. It will be a much happier occasion and all her troubles will be a distant memory to be forgotten and laid to rest."

The two spirits embraced each other lovingly before they drifted gracefully into the sparkling mists of the crystal ethers.

About the Author

Jinna was born off the East coast of Sumatra in Indonesia. She has made her home in Canada since 1967 and lives with her husband in a small community in Northern Ontario, Canada.

She is a twice ordained Minister. A Metaphysical minister ordained by Lightworker and a Spiritual Minister registered under the International Assembly of Spiritual Healers and Earth Stewards.

She is a Reiki Master and certified in numerous energy healing modalities such as EMF, IET, Healing Touch, and Acu Touch etc. She is a Spiritual Counselor and a certified instructor for the Spiritual Psychology course. She continues to offer many classes and workshops in her home or where ever she is invited to do so.

Jinna is the Founder of the New Energy Healing modality coined EHF (Energy Healing Facilitator) This modality was channeled through the Quan Yin Energy and she was guided to introduce this course in numerous cities in Canada and in the United States. Teaching and learning continue to be her passion and it is a major part of her everyday life.

About the Cover Art Illustrator

Carlos Rubio is a Columbian-born multi-talented Canadian artist who, after having explored the engineering field, decided to shift direction towards the artistic stream.

He graduated as a graphic designer in Toronto and is currently working as a professional in this field. He continues with his passion in painting and illustration during his leisure time. He has produced a number of exceptional pieces for private viewing only at this time.